Deceived

Claire Hollis, Ph.D.

Claire Hollis, Ph.D.

Deceived

ISBN 0-9673122-4-8

Library of Congress Catalog Card Number: 99-096604

Copyright © 1999 by Claire Hollis

Printed in the United States of America

Published by   Warfare Publications
                     PMB#206
                     4577 Gunn Highway
                     Tampa, FL 33624 USA
                     (813) 265-2379
                     Fax: (813) 908-0228
                     E-mail: WarfareP@aol.com
                     Web site: www.warfareplus.com

Unless otherwise indicated, all scripture references are from the authorized *King James Version* of the Bible.

Deceived is the third book of the series.

DEDICATION

To my husband, Paul, whom God has chosen, anointed, and called to be a general in His end-time army. I praise God that He has allowed me to be joined with him in a spiritual union with the same call on our lives, and the same goal of doing warfare on a daily basis for *our* Leader, whose archenemy is the devil.

A
Note From
The Author

This book is prophetic in nature. It is a fictitious account of what could happen soon on planet earth based on Bible prophecy. **Deceived** is the third book of a series in which JJ and Lynn Murphy again find themselves in life threatening situations. President Catlin and Bishop John have been successful at deceiving most of the world by pretending to be holy and religious, and performing miracles. Now, JJ and Lynn have to make the decision to either obey President Catlin by receiving the computer chip stamped on their forehead or hand, or to die.

The story begins in **The Light** when JJ and Lynn Murphy visit their nephew in the mysterious little town of Centerville. They uncover demonic secrets that have remained hidden for years. Rulers of the dark world retaliate by issuing a death contract against them.

In the second book of the series, *Delayed Invasion,* JJ and Lynn Murphy go to Washington, D.C. to get the book, *This Means War,* published that they wrote while in Centerville. While there, they discover that a U.S. military crew stationed in Germany mysteriously intercepts a plot to overthrow the governments of the world by disguising themselves as beings from outer space. JJ and Lynn witness a kidnapping which puts them in the middle of this top-secret invasion plan.

A forthcoming book, *Wrath,* is being written that will continue this chain of events to the climax and the end of time as we know it. JJ and Lynn have been entertaining two house guests who unleash supernatural powers that far exceed that of Bishop John and President Catlin.

I recommend that you read all of the books to really get to know and appreciate the main characters, and to receive the full impact of the story.

Claire Hollis, Ph.D.

Claire Hollis, Ph.D.

Deceived

1

S omewhere in the second heaven was a room, where no human had ever been, thick with an ominous presence. The only light present was emitted from the small flames that burned endlessly around the perimeter of the room. A long, black table stretched through the center of the room with Satan, himself, stationed at one end. The stagnant air reeked of an unidentifiable stench.

It was a very concealed place, for it was Satan's headquarters, and only the few elite ever gained access to it. Demons could enter into the outer courts, but only those who were invited were allowed into this unholy room. And, if for some reason, one was summoned to this obscure sanctuary, it was usually accompanied with great fear and trembling.

Suddenly, the only door to the room slowly opened. A petite woman entered, with two escorts in long black robes trailing behind her. The escorts' heads were covered with hoods, and all that could be seen were their piercing eyes, sunken back into their sockets.

Lana was always seen in either red or black outfits that were excellent in taste, expensive, and basic. She was tiny in stature and wore bright, blood-red lipstick. Her cold black hair was pulled back into a bun, which exposed the large cluster of diamond earrings she always wore. Today she was wearing black, matching her black eyes which darted back and forth as she grinned mischievously.

The two henchmen stopped at the opening of the room and fell down on their faces in reverence. As Lana entered, she bowed low in a worshipful manner until Satan released her to have a seat at the table.

"Lana, I have a plan that's indestructible!" Satan declared, as he leaned forward with both fists on the table. His gnarly voice was a distorted imitation of that of a human's. "You've heard the expression, 'If you can't beat 'em, join 'em!' Well, that's exactly what we're going to do!"

He tightened his lips in disgust before he continued. "We can't seem to get rid of this revival that's sweeping the world because of the book that JJ and Lynn Murphy wrote, *This Means War*. People are being 'born again' by the thousands on a daily basis. Then, they are ridding themselves of the demon spirits that we have strategically placed in them!"

"Well then, what can we do?" Lana inquired.

Satan jumped up, sending the chair behind him crashing to the floor. "How can you be so stupid, Lana? It's as plain as the nose on that human face that you are operating out of!" He screamed. Meanwhile, one of the henchmen who had arrived with Lana scurried over to set Satan's chair upright.

"The answer is very simple: it is called 'Deceit,'" Satan sneered. He then walked around to the back of her chair, grabbed it and swung it around so he was once again in her face. "Lana, you seem to forget that it was *I* who was able to deceive one third of God's angels. It was *I* who developed that master plan, and let me tell you, *it wasn't easy!*" His sour breath blew heavily into Lana's face who sat paralyzed before him.

Satan stood and threw his hands up in the air in victory. "They all knew God personally, face to face. They lived in the glory of pure love, truth, worship and complete protection, and *I* was able to turn their affections and worship from God to *myself.*" He looked up into nowhere as he brought his hands to his chest with elbows still raised. Suddenly, he glanced at Lana. "You should know, Lana," Satan smirked, "you were kicked out of Heaven with all of the rest of us."

Lana shifted uneasily, still not comfortable saying anything.

"Convincing the angels to follow me was extremely difficult," Satan continued. "However, these humans – HA! Give me a break, Lana! Deceiving humans is the easiest thing that I've ever done! It hardly takes any effort." He began to walk around the table as his voice raised in excitement.

"It was so easy to deceive those first two, Eve, and then Adam. And, we have been at it ever since," he remarked triumphantly.

By this time, Satan was once again at the end of the table where the henchman remained at attention with his seat prepared. Satan sat down and the henchman stepped away. He leaned back in his chair as Lana swiveled her chair back around to face him.

"I will have to admit, though," Satan muttered in a lower tone, "this JJ and his goody-goody wife, Lynn, have become quite a challenge to me."

Lana sat silent, never daring to take her eyes off Satan. Knowing what he was capable of doing, she was unsure of her response, so she just listened.

"Lana, I am the master of lies and deceit." He leaned forward on the table, his eyes piercing straight into hers. "Now, listen closely to this ingenious plan because I am appointing you to be the one to carry it out to its completion. *You* will be responsible for the success of this mission, and I do mean *it will be successful.*" Satan paused meaningfully, allowing his words to sink into Lana's understanding. "Here it is…"

"We are going to join this revival of Christianity that is spreading throughout the earth," Satan continued. "God is manifesting His glory through signs and wonders right now all over the world."

"Here's the dilemma," he explained. "Creation only comes from God; however, I am *the expert* at counterfeiting what has already been created. Almost anything God can do, I can forge. I am the master at imitating the real thing. These humans will never know the difference," Satan laughed. "How easy this will be! It will be so easy to perform miracles of healing. All we have to do is tell our spirits of infirmity to back off, and *bingo!* Immediately that person is healed!" He was getting excited again.

Satan suddenly became very serious, as he was about to unfold the details of his master plan. "Lana, I want you to get a couple of high-profile young men; one in the political arena, and one in the religious. We will empower them to do great miracles, and get all of those silly little humans to follow them.

"Then, *when the time is right*, I will enter into one of them, just like I did Judas Iscariot." Satan's eyes grew larger as they burned black and red. His voice growled deep more like that of an animal's than of a human's. "Lana, *I will rule this earth*, and everyone *will* worship *me* or *DIE!*"

His eyes shrunk down to normal and the red disappeared as he softly grabbed Lana's hand. He once again sounded like a human. "If you do a good job on this project, Lana, I just might let you rule with me." He then cupped her face with his hand. " I will give you all of the powers you need to accomplish this mission. Think about it. You could be considered the 'First Lady' of the Universe!"

At that thought, Satan threw himself back in his chair and sent out a chilling laugh. Lana's eyes burned red as she straightened high in her chair with her shoulders back. To finally rule the world! It was about time...

Her thoughts were interrupted as Satan warned, "I will be watching your every move, so don't mess up! This is your final chance, don't blow it!" His eyes were growing large and were burning black and red again. Satan pointed to the door and growled loudly, "Now, go!"

Lana stood up, lowered her head, and bowed while backing to the door. Once at the door, she briskly turned on her heel, and with her head held high, she exited the room. A henchman quickly shut the door. Lana stood there for a moment reveling in her own glory. Then, glaring at the surrounding henchmen, she stuck out a long, bony finger covered with blood red nail polish and pointed it at them. Something like electricity lunged from her fingertips and stunned the henchmen, thrusting them into the wall. They screamed in pain. Lana lowered her finger, which released them and sent them falling into a heap on the floor. Immediately, they cowered before her in submission with their faces to the ground.

Lana threw her head back and laughed. She threw her hands up in the air like she had seen Satan do, as she began to strut down the long hall. Pride had gripped her again. "Just think," Lana whispered to herself, "*I* am the one that Master Satan has chosen to reign with. *I am the One!*"

Lana's eyes burned red and black as she marched forth, determined to rule the world.

Deceived

2

As Lana was returning to the earth, she looked at the planet in complete disgust. As the humans accepted Jesus Christ as their personal Savior, becoming born again, a beam of light from heaven would enter into them. The natural eye could not see this light; but in the spiritual realm, all could see it. One would have thought that it was a Fourth of July celebration the way these beams of light were being sent down in every direction. "This is so repulsive," Lana thought. "If I wanted to see a laser light show, I'd go to an amusement park."

"This plan cannot fail!" She continued to murmur under her breath. "Satan is the chief of deception, and I know he will eventually win over the other two thirds of the angels. He just has to! Then, we will overthrow God! HA!" She threw her fist in defiance towards the heavens.

Lana began to lay out her strategy. She needed to get two men; a politician and a clergyman. It actually would not be that difficult. There were so many of them to choose from who were already filled with pride, greed, lust, and jealousy that deceiving them would be a piece of cake.

"This will be fun," Lana chuckled to herself. "I am going to like this assignment. I *will* come up with the best." She gloated. "Satan can trust me with this because *I am* the best!"

Lana immediately called together a meeting to be held the next morning at 10:00am with her top Stronghold Spirits. It was at a new headquarters, and all thirteen had gathered one hour early to await the arrival of Lana. Some were irritated at the change of locations.

"I don't like it here in this new meeting place! There are Christians everywhere. I am just not comfortable with this at all!" One of the thirteen said.

Another one slammed the table where they were sitting with his fists and said, "I loathe that JJ and Lynn Murphy! If it weren't for them, we would still be in Centerville where there wasn't any light. I really liked that place. It was not intimidating."

About that time, someone said, "*Sshh*! She's close by. I can sense her presence." There was dead silence as Lana came through the wall right behind the head of the table. This was not the normal Lana. Usually, her fangs were showing and she would be snorting and snarling at them. Today, however, she was all smiles and very spirited.

"Ladies and Gentlemen," Lana began. "Well, that's what you appear to be anyway…" Lana paused to laugh at her own joke. Since no one responded, she continued, "I've got great news for you! We have a plan that cannot fail. We are going to 'cash in' on this world-wide revival." She pranced before them in great excitement.

"Just when we thought that things were hopeless, our great Leader has developed a fool-proof plan." Lana stopped to make sure she had their undivided attention. Still standing, she put both hands on the table and leaned towards them. Then, dramatically, she announced:

"WE ARE GOING TO JOIN THEM!"

Gasps could be heard from everyone in the room. Their faces displayed looks of puzzlement. Lana repeated herself, "That's right! We are going to join them!

"We have been given unlimited powers to show signs and wonders," Lana explained. "We can counterfeit whatever these men and women of God are doing through God's power. Haven't we done it before? Remember a long time ago, how much fun we had with Moses and Pharaoh? This is going to be 'party time,' so get excited! Satan is preparing to take over. The time is finally here, and we'll all rule with him!"

A stir of excitement passed through the group as they exchanged glances with one another. Their evil grins fueled Lana's energy as she continued.

"So, what we are going to do is infiltrate among the Christians and counterfeit everything that they are doing. The only difference is that everything they do is through the power of God, and everything we do is through Satan's deception.

"Now..." Lana sat down at the head of the table and leaned back in her chair identical to the way she had seen Satan do just the day before, "we will need two humans through whom we will work our strategy. I want you all to go out on a witch-hunt..." Lana stopped and laughed. "Get it? A witch hunt? Ha! Ha! Oh, well, you get the idea!" The group snickered respectfully but still remained unsure as to what she was trying to say. Lana continued, "Each of you are to use your resources and find me two young men as our candidates. Now listen closely to the criteria." Lana leaned forward to accentuate her point.

"I need a man in politics, and I need a man of the cloth. They need to be full of charisma, and very well respected. Make sure they are full of pride and greed, and don't have a problem lying or cheating. If they struggle with adultery and lust, that's an added bonus. Look for the ones who can take the Word of God and distort it to say what they want it to, and who can twist the law in order to get what they want. After the two finalists are selected, they will receive great power from Satan himself."

Lana stood up suddenly, sending her chair crashing to the floor, just like she had seen Satan do. She pointed to the door. "Now, go!" She commanded. "We will meet back here one week from today, and I expect to hear some good reports!" She turned on her heel and disappeared through the wall.

The group sat silent for a moment, still stunned by their new assignment. As the realization began to sink in, one could see the competition beginning to mount as they began to declare who would come forth with the perfect candidates. Each one was certain their territory contained the "chosen ones" for this assignment, which would then esteem them more highly than the rest.

Meanwhile, the Word of God was sweeping through the world with great force. Everywhere people were witnessing about the wonderful things of the Lord. Sick bodies were being totally restored by the thousands. Christians were commanding demons to leave people in the name of Jesus. Miracles were occurring every-where; people of all nations and tribes were uniting as one with Jesus being their common denominator.

The days of the "Superstar" preachers were over as knowledge and understanding of the Word of God greatly increased to every believer. People of every social structure and class were spreading the gospel. Small groups were meeting in neighborhoods and homes throughout the world. It went beyond social, religious, and racial classes. Christians were binding together, sharing with each other, and there was much peace, joy, and happiness.

Claire Hollis, Ph.D.

Deceived

3

J and Lynn Murphy were relaxing quietly in their home when they heard the doorbell ring. Their cocker spaniel, Dudley, heard the doorbell, too, and began to bark. Almost instantly, his mate and all of the puppies were also barking, breaking the silence.

Lynn walked over to the door and opened it. Tim Perry from down the street was standing there, anxious and out of breath. He quickly proceeded past small pleasantries, getting straight to the point.

"Can you and JJ please come to my house right away? There is a man there who has just prayed and received Jesus Christ into his life as his personal Savior. The demons that are inhabiting him are mad, and they are in an uproar. They are thrashing him around the room; and they are putting up a terrible fight." Tim stopped to catch his breath before continuing, "We can't seem to do anything about it, and we need your help!"

By this time, JJ had joined Lynn at the door and had heard everything that Tim said. Without saying a word, they nodded to each other in agreement as JJ grabbed their jackets out of the closet. Within minutes, they were out of the house, leaving behind a family of bewildered cocker spaniels staring at a closed door.

Tim led JJ and Lynn into his house. About fifteen people were lined up against the walls of the living room, as a man stood bent over in the center of the room, snarling and growling. JJ went forward and asked him his name.

Someone in the room answered, "Michael Robbins."

JJ slowly stepped closer to the man, and gently asked, "Who did you come here with, Michael?" The man immediately snapped out of it and was back to himself.

Tim stepped forward and introduced Michael to JJ and Lynn. They proceeded to tell Michael how he had been behaving. Michael responded with shock. JJ explained to him that a demon had temporary control of him, and that they were going to make it leave. Michael's strength suddenly left his legs and he collapsed onto a nearby couch. JJ sat down beside him.

"That demon spirit must have a legal right to do what he just did, Michael," JJ slowly explained. "Satan and his kingdom are legalists, and if they have a legal right to torment you, they will." He paused for a moment. "Michael, the Bible teaches us that Satan has a legal right to torment us if we have unforgiveness in our hearts. Tell me, who has done you wrong?"

Michael sat up. He tightened his jaws, clenched his teeth, and glared straight at the ceiling.

"It's my father! I hate him!" Michael shouted. "He killed my mother. I watched him do it. I was only seven at the time. They had been fighting while he was drunk. He went to the kitchen and grabbed a knife out of the drawer. Then he stabbed her, and stabbed her, and stabbed her..." Michael choked back a sob. His shoulders slumped forward, and he dropped his head into his hands. He began to rub his fists into his eyes as if trying to dispel the memory. Two minutes of total silence passed before he looked up and turned to JJ. "I have never spoken to him since that day." Michael's eyes grew hard as he continued, "I was left alone, and the state sent me from family to family; no one ever wanted me. My dad is currently in the prison at Scottsdale. I have always said that when he gets out, I will do to him what he did to my mom!" He choked back another sob. He dropped his face back into his hands.

JJ gently put his arm around Michael. Sounds of sniffles could be heard throughout the room, and there wasn't a dry eye in the house. The people who were moments before clinging to the sides of the room began to quietly sit down in surrounding chairs or on the floor.

"Michael, let me explain something to you," JJ said gently. "People are beautiful, but devils are ugly. Your dad is a beautiful person that God loves, and even sent his son, Jesus, to die for. But, somewhere along the way, your father opened the door to allow some devils to come into his life. Devils are rude guests. They don't leave until they are kicked out. It could be that they could have come down through the ancestral line." JJ paused to let that sink in. "You know people die, but demons don't; they just look for new homes."

Michael looked up at the wall for a moment, deep in thought. He then turned to JJ and said, "My grandfather was a hit man in the mafia, and my great-grandfather was from a tribe of Indians who participated in a lot of massacres. Do you think that had any bearing on what my dad did?"

JJ reached over to the coffee table and picked up a Bible that was lying there. He answered Michael by saying, "Of course, and there could be even more things involved. It could be that your father had experienced a lot of rejection. Maybe your mother also rejected him, and he couldn't handle it. Understand me, I am not justifying anything. What he did was definitely wrong; however, he may have been set up to do it."

JJ continued, "The demonic kingdom came here to this earth with the ultimate goal to kill, steal, and destroy. They intentionally create circumstances to occur in people's lives which would provoke them to either kill someone or to commit suicide. That's the demons' job, and they are very good at what they do." JJ shook his head and let out a "humph" before continuing, "They don't always succeed in getting a person to the point of murder or suicide, but that *is* their ultimate plan."

Michael began to soften. "I just remembered some-thing. I haven't thought about it in all of these years, but my little friend told me something that he overheard his mom and dad say. They said that my mom deserved what she got for letting her boyfriend get her pregnant…" Michael swallowed the lump in his throat as he stared in realization at JJ. His eyes quickly formed large pools of tears. He suddenly buried his face in his hands again as a flood of emotions broke through the mental dam he had so safely constructed years ago. Michael began to wail like a baby.

JJ continued to rest one arm around Michael, and with the other arm, he made a gesture to the other people in the room. With his mouth, he silently motioned for them to pray. He then leaned close to Michael and said, "Michael, the spirit of rejection and murder is on you, too. The devil set you up by having all those families reject you. Hate and revenge has eaten away at you from the murderous scene that you witnessed. Because of that, you have become hard on the inside. Let's get rid of this thing." JJ squeezed Michael's shoulder gently. "Let's get it out of your life right now!"

Michael plopped down and leaned his head back. Drained from the emotions, he closed his eyes and dropped his arms to his sides. He relaxed there for a moment before he opened his eyes and glanced at JJ.

"You're right, I have been bitter; but I don't know what to do to get rid of the anger."

"Michael," JJ responded, "I want you to deliberately choose with your free will to forgive your father. Don't go by your feelings; just go by what the Word of God tells us to do." He laid the Bible on his lap and, with one hand, flipped it open to the New Testament.

JJ continued, "Michael, the Bible is very clear about forgiveness. It says in Matthew chapter six, verses fourteen and fifteen that *'if ye forgive men their trespasses, your heavenly Father will also forgive you: But if ye forgive not men their trespasses, neither will your Father forgive your trespasses.'*

"So, you can see how important it is that we forgive people. I want you to say it out loud so Satan and his kingdom can hear you. You see, devils can't read your mind, but they can hear what you say. They need to hear you say it. I also want you to release the judgment that you have had against your father."

Michael sat up again, his attention focused on what JJ was saying. A look of determination covered his face.

"Okay…" Michael said slowly. JJ nodded at Michael, encouraging him to pray.

Every head in the room was bowed as Michael quietly began to pray. His voice broke several times as he forgave his father for all that he had done to him, and to release the judgment that he had held in his heart all of these years. As he prayed, the tears continued to flow from Michael's eyes.

When Michael had finished praying, JJ moved off of the couch, and got down on his knees in front of Michael. Gently resting his hands on Michael's shoulders, JJ firmly said, "In the name of Jesus, I now break any ungodly emotional soul ties between Michael and his father, and his father's ancestors. You spirits of rejection, revenge, hate, bitterness, *come out of him now, in the name of Jesus*! I command you to go now into uninhabited places!"

A terrifying scream escaped from Michael and his eyes bulged out from their sockets. His body suddenly began to shake uncontrollably. Quickly it was over, and Michael collapsed back into the couch. Absolute silence filled the room.

The room was so holy one could actually feel God's presence. The silence was broken as Michael began to laugh with tears streaming down his face.

"I've never in my life felt so free. I feel like a thousand pounds has just been lifted off my back!" His hands went up in the air as a sign of surrender and praise to God who has all power over the devil and his kingdom.

Michael threw his arms around JJ, who returned the embrace with excitement. By this time, everyone in the room was standing, clapping, and shouting praises to God. The cheering in the room led one of the ladies to burst out into a song, and instantly the room was filled with singing. The air was thick with the presence of God.

Tim's wife, Penny, who had some food prepared, began to serve refreshments to her guests. Some of the ladies assisted her in bringing platters of cookies and finger foods to the dining room table, which was adorned with a beautiful bouquet of fresh flowers placed in the center. It was quite a feast that Penny presented to the group. Everyone enjoyed a wonderful time of fellowship as they delighted in Michael's deliverance. It was a joyful celebration.

After indulging in all of Penny's scrumptious treats, JJ and Lynn gathered up their jackets preparing to go home. Michael rushed over to JJ and said, "I have decided to go see my father tomorrow in Scottsdale."

JJ grabbed Michael's arm, and squeezed it reassuringly, "Be sure to bind up any demon spirits, in Jesus' name, that could be active around your father before you get there. Dispatch angels to encamp around you, and ask God to guard your mouth so that you will only say what the Holy Spirit wants you to say."

Michael nodded, and smiled. Hugging JJ, he said, "Thank you so much for all of your help."

As JJ and Lynn merrily walked hand-in-hand down the sidewalk to their home and awaiting cocker spaniels, Lynn said, "Did you notice? Michael didn't even look like the same person we saw when we first entered Tim's house?"

While JJ nodded and smiled back at Lynn, Lana was somewhere off in the distance slamming her briefcase around in anger; another beam of light had been transmitted to earth from Heaven.

Deceived

4

Exactly one week had passed since Lana had met with her top council of thirteen and had commissioned them with their assignment. The group had already assembled and was again awaiting Lana's arrival; only this time, there was silence. Each sat at the conference table eyeing one another curiously, wondering who would come forth with the chosen ones. The usual bantering was gone since everyone was so absorbed in his own selfish thoughts that no one felt like engaging in conversation. They were consumed with the hope of their nominees being the chosen ones because they loved recognition.

Lana suddenly burst into the room with a commanding air of confidence. Since she was expecting positive results from today's meeting, she had decided to wear red. Her black eyes were flashing, and her red lipstick was much too bright. It reminded them of the blood of her victims.

Lana threw her black briefcase up on the table, clicked on a few buttons, and threw the lid back. Without saying a word, she grabbed a pen from inside and jotted down a few notes. Keeping a few papers in her hand, Lana then slid the pen into its slot, grabbed the top of the briefcase and slammed the lid back down as the locks clicked into place. She carefully eyed each one of them slowly as she said, "Good morning, and how are we all doing today?" Her cynical smile betrayed her pleasantries.

A few muttered some replies, although nobody was interested in small talk. They were eager to present their candidates.

"I have been waiting for today!" Lana slammed her fist onto her briefcase. "I trust that you will provide me with the two candidates that I need to take over the government and manipulate the religious system for our master plan." She walked around to the corner of the conference table and slapped the guy sitting there on the back.

"Let's start with you!" Lana commanded.

The man stood haughtily to his feet. He was the captain over the demons of pride, selfishness, stubbornness, competition, and gossip. Staring straight ahead, he said, "Master Lana, the two men that I have chosen are two that we have complete control of. We have been setting them up since they were small children." He smiled. "Right now, they have so much pride that they think they are God. They would do anything, and I mean anything, in order to control the world. They are so self-righteous, especially the religious one. He has all the big time TV star preachers as his friends, and he would do anything to become more popular than they are. We have competition flowing like a river into these fellows. It's so funny to sit back and watch them perform. They are so self-righteous that they spend most of their day looking in a mirror. Let me tell you who they are…"

"Stop!" Lana cut him off. "Let's have some fun with this." She walked briskly to her briefcase and grabbed the stack of papers that she had kept out. Handing them to the captain who was still standing, she said, "Don't say who your candidates are. Instead, write them on these papers, one for the religious man, and one for the political man. Then, I will stack them in two piles and we will see who our winners are." She snickered her approval at such a great idea, as the other thirteen glanced around with great excitement. This *was* going to be fun.

Up popped the next "person." "Sorry, Ladies and Gentlemen, and I use those words loosely!" He chuckled under his breath. "I have you all beat! I have two men who stand out far above the others." He scribbled the names down on his sheets of paper before continuing. "As you know, I am in charge of mental illness, insanity, double-mindedness, and multiple personalities. Well, I have two men that stand out far above the others. Our group has programmed them with so many multiple personalities that the real humans don't even know who they are any more! We have complete control of each personality, and we can choose at will which one we want to activate at any given time. My choices are surely going to win," he declared as he handed his papers to Lana.

"No, no, no!" The third one at the table refuted. "I am in charge of the mind spirits, and I have two men that we can control at all times. We can bind up their mind, make them go into a trance, forget things, cause them to daydream, or even to fall asleep," He wrote his two names down. "In fact, we have their minds so bound up that they will never accept the message of Jesus Christ. I know that Lana will choose my men."

The one in charge of familiar spirits quickly spoke up. "The two men that I have carefully picked out from these humans have dabbled around in just about everything we have to offer in the occult. As little boys, we got them started with the Ouija board. They began to call on us, and within seconds, we were there to do their bidding. They are intrigued with our world and are quite knowledgeable of the powers that accompany it. They have sacrificed babies, made potions, and now they are into this 'new age' stuff, burning candles, incense, and so forth. They love the power!" He laughed hysterically. "We even had them worshiping a statue made by man! I *know* my candidates are the ones!"

A fifth captain jumped into the conversation. "Master Lana, you know that I control the spirits of fear. I have to tell you, the two men that I have chosen are so afraid of not doing what we tell them to do, it is incredible. They portray themselves as being confident and in control, but they're not. We are!" He pointed both of his thumbs to his chest, and threw his shoulders and head back with great pride as he continued, "We put terrorizing thoughts into their minds, and immediately their heart rate jumps, their pulse increases and they begin to perspire. We have complete control of them, and they will never disappoint us. Here are my entries." He handed his papers over to Lana, who snatched them quickly and read over the names.

Lana's countenance began to change as she took a peak at the names. Her piercing eyes beamed red, and her fangs showed through an evil smirk. Lana began to laugh roughly, which burst into a screeching cackle. Her head began to shake uncontrollably, and the pins in her hair worked themselves free, flying wildly through the air. Those around her were dodging the pins frantically.

The council members glanced at each other confoundedly and took this as a good sign that they were succeeding in their plot. They began to snicker as well.

Lana suddenly regained her composure, returned to her human state, and looked expectantly to the sixth member at the table. He quickly arose.

"I am in charge of the sad spirits," He said. "We cause these earthlings to feel rejected, lonely, and to have depression, grief, guilt and despair." He rubbed his hands together gleefully. "Although both of the men that I have chosen do not appear to be depressed in public, when they are alone, they can barely cope with life. They have to be around people all of the time in order to function.

"We got an early start with both men by causing their fathers to reject them. Then, we set people up all of their lives to reject them. First, it was a schoolteacher, then friends, then a girl friend, and

31

finally the spouse. They have so much rejection that they will do anything, and I mean *anything,* to get attention.

"They both have such hatred for their fathers, that it has caused them to hate everyone. They use people to get what they want, and their feelings are as cold as ice. They have no respect for life."

He scratched out some names on his sheets of paper, folded them, and slid them down the table to Lana. She glanced quickly at them before adding them to her stacks. She smirked before turning to the other side of the u-shaped conference table. They were halfway through the nominations, and Lana was already pleased with the results.

Lana nodded expectantly to the next member of the group. He stood up and began his dissertation.

"I hate to disappoint all of you, but there is no way your candidates will win, when mine are perfect," he said. "My group specializes in jealousy, bitterness, revenge, anger, and murder.

"We began with each man as a small boy, and we had their mothers choose a favorite, and guess what? It wasn't them. We had the mothers give all of the love and attention and the best of everything to their siblings. We made sure that they always got punished for what their brothers did. The jealousy began at home, just like it did with Cain and Abel.

"Remember when God didn't accept Cain's sacrifice, and how we got him to become bitter, not only with God, but with his brother, too? We have been able to plant in my two entries the same spirit of jealousy that we planted in Cain. They have both gone out in a fit of rage and murdered someone. No other human knows about it, but we could tell by their reactions that they enjoyed it."

He walked proudly to the head of the table, laid his votes onto the stacks, and turned to go back to his seat. So absorbed into his own thoughts, he didn't notice the next member of the group rising from his chair, purposely bumping into him as he passed by.

"Hey! Watch it!" He declared angrily, and turned to the group. "Did you see that? He tried to knock me over!" He pushed the guy in the arm, and accused, "You did that on purpose!"

"Did not! I don't know what you are talking about!" The other guy denied.

Lana loved it! She just sat there and grinned, for she knew that he was in charge of the spirits of lying. Feeling in complete control, she commanded, "Continue on!"

Both men glared at each other before the captain of jealousy sat down, while the captain of lying stood straight up. Focusing his gaze directly at Lana, he said, "Master Lana, my group has two men who are perfect for this position. The politician can lie better than anyone on the planet. He is so deceitful that he could even fool us! He gets anything he wants, and knows how to use the laws of the land to twist them around to say what he wants. He seldom ever tells the truth.

"And the religious one—let me tell you about him!" He continued excitedly. "He gets up in his pulpit and tells just enough truth, and quotes enough of the scriptures to sound believable. He knows the right words to say, and prays these absolutely fabulous prayers. He is so good looking that he's in love with himself.

"He looks and sounds like a holy man of God, when in fact, he's actually just like us. You know we've been called a 'wolf in sheep's clothing' and 'angels of light'? Well, let me tell you that this guy has us all beat. He can have an audience eating out of his hands in minutes. He has deceived people into thinking that he gets his power from God, when in fact, he *knows* that *we* are giving it to him. He's already popular, so therefore, half of the work is already done. We don't have to groom someone for this position – we've already done that!"

Someone from across the table muttered, "How can we believe him? He never tells the truth!" A few snickers were heard throughout the room.

Lana burst out into that screeching cackle that made them all want to put their hands over their ears, but the fear of what she would do to them was far to great to move an inch. The one in charge of the lying deceitful spirits was disgusted with the whole bunch as he took his votes to the head of table.

The "woman" who headed up the group of Anti-christ spirits spoke up. "My group has spent the whole week going over our most prized possessions. There are so many to choose from, but after much deliberation, we have come up with two perfect men for these positions.

"These men really are *against* Christ. They are steeped into witchcraft, rebellion, and self-exaltation.

"Satan wouldn't have a problem ruling the world through them. They're on our side, and are eager to satisfy us in any way they can. It's so funny - the political figure won't make a single decision without consulting us through a witch, Satanist, or palm reader. He keeps a psychic on staff so that she's available to him at all times. The first thing he does every day is to look at his horoscope, and without our advisor, he won't make a move."

She strolled over to Lana and handed her the names.

Lana was enjoying this. She nodded to the next member at the table, "Cathy, you are next. Let's hear who the spirits of poverty have come up with."

Cathy bowed her head and sighed. Without looking at Lana, she slowly spoke, "Master Lana, we've been so busy stealing time, money, love, spiritual growth, health, peace, and joy from the humans that we didn't have time to do the homework. I don't have anyone to present to you."

Everyone looked at each other in sheer terror. It was deathly quiet in the room. No one dared to even move as all were waiting for Lana to blow up in anger and do bodily harm, like they had seen her do before on numerous occasions.

Although it had seemed like hours had passed, it was only minutes before Lana opened her mouth to speak. "That's okay, don't worry about it," she replied. The council sat in total disbelief. This was a first! They were all perplexed as to why she was in such a good mood.

The captain of the spirits of bondage quickly responded. Trying to re-establish the flow of the meeting, he immediately began to describe his two nominees. "My two choices are in bondage to us; we've had them dependent on some kind of a drug since they were adolescent. They are both so addicted, that they don't make a decision without the drugs that we provide; we control them with the drugs," he stated. "We have chosen the best that we have to offer you." He slid his papers over to Lana.

The old man who was in charge of the spirits of infirmity was rubbing his hands together as he stood.

"Master Lana, it was a very difficult decision for us to make," he said. "You see, we have almost every human in our control; and in the two men that I have chosen for you, we have impregnated almost every sickness or disease available. They are currently lying dormant. These men are experiencing excellent health, but all we have to do is activate anything you want; they can be dead in seconds at your command," he explained. His names were passed over to Lana.

There were only two people left to vote, and they both stood up together.

"Master Lana," one of them began. "We decided to work on this project together because Mary is in charge of whoredom, and I am in charge of perversion, and we are constantly crossing paths with each other in these silly little human's lives."

Mary spoke up, "God made human reproductive organs to bind married couples together, to 'make them one,' and to produce life, which He intended on being a beautiful experience." She glanced at her accomplice. "We, however, have been very successful at perverting it, and causing it to become very ugly! We've used that sexual drive in mankind to destroy marriages, families, churches, governments, and nations.

"The two men that we've chosen are so driven by their perverted sexual desires that they are completely out of control, *which means that we are in control*!" Mary continued. "These two humans are like dogs on a leash, and we control the leash!" Mary turned to her partner and they snickered at each other. They handed in their papers to Lana before they both sat down.

All the votes were in. Each one sat in suspense as Lana once more shuffled through the papers, as if to double-check each one. She was quiet for a long time; she delighted in teasing them. They were spell bound and afraid to breathe for fear of breaking the silence. She silently stood to her feet, smirking in satisfaction.

Suddenly, Lana threw the papers high into the air, scattering them throughout the room as she twirled around in delight. Her arms grew out long like a gorilla's and almost touched the floor as she frantically waved them about, while cackling loudly. She looked more like a monkey than she did a human. After jumping up and down and beating on her chest for two minutes, Lana turned to the awaiting group of onlookers. They watched as she returned to her original appearance.

"You have all given me the names of the same two men!" Lana shouted exuberantly. "It is unanimous! We don't even need to vote. These two have to be the greatest!"

The council members all looked at each other in pure disbelief. They were completely shocked. It wasn't any wonder that they were all so certain that each had the perfect candidate - because each did!

The room was instantly filled with great squealing, grunting, and howling. They continued to celebrate for approximately twenty more minutes when, suddenly, the room was charged with something like electricity as an ominous presence entered the room. Lana twirled around in great surprise to inspect the unexpected visitor, only to find herself staring into two large piercing eyes. She was beholding the very face of Satan.

Deceived

5

L ana and all thirteen members of the council immediately threw themselves on the floor in worship before him. Because he seldom left his headquarters, it was very unusual for Satan to make an appearance, even to his top council members. This was a rare occasion.

Satan stood there for nearly an hour, basking in his own glory as he listened to them sing their praises to him. He loved it! Although he wanted to quickly get back to his headquarters, he couldn't resist the temptation to be worshiped. That seemed to empower him.

Finally, Satan motioned for Lana to get up, moving on to his purpose for being there. Lana quickly rose to her feet and sat in the chair that Satan had pointed to. The council members remained prostrate on the floor.

"Have you made a decision?" Satan questioned Lana.

Lana bowed her head low, "Yes, Master, we have come to a unanimous decision on the perfect candidates for this job." She looked up at Satan and said, "We have chosen Prime Minister Catlin and Bishop John as our vessels."

Satan stared intently at Lana for a brief moment before a wicked smile appeared on his face. Evil ambitions already filled his thoughts when he replied, "Very good! Excellent! I'm very pleased!

"Now, I need you all to join this revival immediately. Don't delay," Satan commanded. "Whatever God is doing, you are to counterfeit. Prepare your armies to become super religious," he sneered. "It's easy for us to counterfeit *healings* since our spirits of infirmity are the ones causing most of the sickness to begin with!" Satan sneered. "All we have to do is tell our demon to back off, and 'boom!' the human has his healing!" His voice dripped with sarcasm.

"Deliverances? Exorcisms?" Satan questioned. "It's the same thing...Just deactivate the demon and the human will think he got rid of it.

"To imitate Godly *prophecies,* just have one of our leaders predict that something is going to happen, and then make sure it does happen, just as it was prophesied. We are already doing that with fortune-telling," Satan said smugly.

"As far as **salvation** is concerned, and accepting Jesus' death for the forgiveness of their sins, *don't let them do that!* Instead, make sure they accept a false Christ by getting them a statue, or some other human to take Christ's place. These humans absolutely **love** worshipping something that they can see. This is a marvelous plan!" Satan was obviously deep in thought. "We're going to get them all to worship Bishop John. After all, he's our winner! That's it! I want all of the *spiritual* people to worship him!"

Lana sat mesmerized in her chair, focused completely on Satan. She did not want to mess this plan up, so therefore, she needed every bit of instruction she could get. Once they would succeed in their mission, she would become the ruler next to Satan, and that was her desire – to rule the universe! Determination was planted solidly within her as she continued to stare at him.

He turned to Lana excitedly. His black eyes burned red. His gnarly mouth let out a burst of foul, hot breath when he declared, *"Miracles* will be easy! Get some of our group to counterfeit God's holy angels and have them appear all over the world. Be sure to have the angels point to Bishop John as having great approval from God. Show a few signs and wonders; those humans will never know the difference. They'll all think it's God.

"Send your groups out and have them float a few objects in the air. Get them to hypnotize some, and make them think that they had a visitation from God, but always make sure that Bishop John is exalted.

"We will have them all following us so fast…"Satan suddenly had a thought. "Why, we may even be able to deceive some of God's angels in the process! Who knows? Ha! Ha! Ha! This is going to be so much fun!" Satan growled in triumph.

"Now, for Prime Minister Catlin," Satan continued on with his instructions. "He's perfect; he's the one that will rule the world. Make sure that everyone loves him, and that he has no enemies. Also, make sure that he has the entire planet under his control.

"*When the time is right, **I will enter into him,*** and receive all of the honor, glory, and worship that these humans are capable of giving."

"Lana," Satan's eyes became like slits as he peered directly at her, "I want you to report to me weekly with your progress." His look intensified as he said, "I am warning you now, you are not to allow that JJ and Lynn Murphy to blotch this up like they did our last plan!

"They have God's protection around them, and we can't touch them. But, I want you to be aware of where they are every minute, and report to me what they are doing. At least we can hinder their plans by influencing the people around them."

Satan gazed at Lana in scrutiny to confirm that she had comprehended his directions. Nodding at him quickly, Lana replied, "It will be done as you say, Master." She threw herself down onto the floor again, prostrate before him. As quickly as he had entered, Satan departed.

Five minutes of complete silence had passed before anyone dared to move. Certain that Satan was not returning, Lana decisively picked herself up off the floor. The other members followed her lead. Even though they were not involved in the conversation, each member had heard every word and didn't need to be given any instructions. They immediately jumped into formulating their strategies. The room was charged with energy because they were so excited.

The Antichrist spirit turned to the captain of anger and revenge and said, "We haven't had this much fun since we killed off all of those Jews a while back. Remember when we set up that plan, and then Satan entered the leader and deployed that great massacre of humans? This sounds like a better party than we had then!"

The captain of anger nodded in agreement as a few of the surrounding members fell on the floor, holding their sides, as they rolled around squealing hysterically in laughter.

It was determined that Lana would visit Bishop John and Prime Minister Catlin to begin priming them for the final strategies. The rest of the group was divided into two halves; one half would infiltrate the "Jesus movement," and the other half would penetrate the political arena.

When the orders were given to begin, one of the members assigned to the political field jeered to the other group, "Our job will be easy because we already control the majority of politicians. Sorry, guys, but while you will be diligently working, we will be having a party!"

The six assigned to the "Jesus movement" had sour looks on their faces and vowed to get revenge. They all truly hated each other.

With their plans in place, Lana dismissed the meeting. Normally, they would meet once a month, but since Satan had placed top priority on this project, it was determined that they would meet weekly.

Lana vanished.

Deceived

6

ishop John was sitting at his desk signing a large stack of papers when suddenly he felt a cold breeze fill the room. He looked up to see a sharply dressed woman in black standing stately before his desk.

"Who are you, and who let you in?" He inquired, startled.

Lana smirked, "Never mind that, Bishop John; I bring you some very good news. First of all, my name is Lana," She confidently held out her right hand toward him. "You will be seeing a lot of me in the days to come."

Bishop John hesitantly leaned forward and grabbed her hand to receive a surprisingly firm handshake.

Unsure of whether to be angry or startled at her unannounced visit, Bishop John remained speechless.

Lana continued, "You have been appointed and groomed to become the leader of the religious world. Can you handle that?" There was a twinkle in her eye as she released his hand from hers.

Bishop John sat up in his chair as he squared his shoulders and straightened his back. A sparkle appeared in his eyes as he replied, "You have come to the right place and are speaking to the right man! Please, tell me more." He extended out his arm to offer her a chair. Lana ignored the invitation as she continued to stand in authority over him.

"Bishop John," Lana began. "You really have no concept of the magnitude of what it is that I am about to tell you. There is currently in the making a *world-wide religion* that will unite every nation under one leader." She placed both of her palms onto his desk with her manicured fingernails outstretched as she slowly leaned her perfectly made-up face forward toward him. Her perfume filled his senses as he tried to focus mentally on her words. Her blood-red lips parted into a smile as she quietly stated, "You are that leader, Bishop John! Everyone will look up to you. You will become one of the most famous men to have ever lived in history.

"I will make that all happen for you," Lana said as she stood back up. "All you need to do is to put me on your staff as your personal assistant immediately."

Bishop John shifted uneasily in his chair. His thoughts were suddenly overcome with desire and lust for power. He nodded in agreement to Lana, still unable to speak.

She continued, "You will have a counter-part who will rule the governments of the world, and you will be his right-hand man."

She paused for a moment. Certain that Bishop John comprehended her words, Lana stated, "Now, I need you to seal this agreement between us. You will do as I say, and I will enable you with supernatural powers. This is a pact which can never be broken...*ever.*" Her chilling gaze bore into the depths of his soul.

Bishop John sat motionless for a moment, contemplating her offer. Overcome with an intense greed for power, he stood up, signifying his affirmation to her words.

Lana held out her right hand, with her palm facing up. Suddenly, a golden goblet filled with a thick red liquid appeared within her hand. Bishop John gawked in astonishment.

"If you are in complete agreement with what I have told you, then drink of this cup," Lana instructed. "As you drink, you will be *filled* with powers that you never knew existed.

"You must tell no one!" Lana warned as she squinted her eyes at him.

Bishop John slowly reached out his shaking hand to take hold of the goblet. Trying to steady it so it wouldn't spill, he grabbed the cup with both hands. Leaning forward, Bishop John placed the goblet to his lips and let the red fluid flow into his mouth. Tipping the goblet up, he gulped every last ounce as blood dripped out of the corners of his mouth and onto his priestly robe. On the last swallow, violent trembling overcame Bishop John as surges of demonic power entered into him.

Lana started to cackle loudly in delight. Curious to see what the strange noise was, the Bishop's secretary opened the door. Bishop John glared at her, and she was instantly thrown back into the hall, slamming her head into the wall behind her. She collapsed onto the floor, unconscious.

Weak with uncontrollable laughter, Lana fell into a chair holding her sides. "You had better learn to control that power of yours, John," she advised, pointing her bony finger at him.

"We will start at eight o'clock sharp in the morning. I am leaving now to see your counter-part, Prime Minister Catlin, whom you will be meeting for dinner tomorrow night."

Lana turned and disappeared through the wall.

Bishop John sank down into his chair, dazed. He leaned forward and dropped his head into his hands. His mind was whirling with questions. Was this all just a dream, or was it real? Was it a vision, or could he have been in a trance? Maybe he didn't get enough sleep last night. Maybe the stresses of life were too great, and beginning to affect his mental capabilities. Whatever it was, it seemed too weird to be true.

He slowly lifted his head and saw the goblet that still remained on his desk. He reached forward to pick it up, expecting it to vanish at his touch. Grasping it between his fingers, he tilted it to find it completely empty. Reliving the last few moments of Lana's visit, he glanced down at his robe to notice the droplets of blood.

Realizing that the stains could arouse suspicion, he immediately headed to the bathroom to wash them off. He made his way around his desk and over to the office door that was ajar. As he entered the hallway, Bishop John saw that his secretary was lying unconscious on the floor, breathing heavily as though she were asleep.

He quickly stepped over her, hurried down the hall into his private bathroom and closed the door behind him. As he turned the faucet, he did a double-take at his reflection in the mirror.

Staring back at him was his own face, the face of Bishop John. However, this man had a golden crown on his head. It was shimmering full of precious stones that sparkled so brightly the whole room was illuminated. Bishop John impulsively reached for the top of his head and to his utter amazement, felt nothing.

"Oh well," he thought, "who cares if it was only an illusion? Someday soon, I will be wearing a crown that the whole world will see, and they will be bowing before me."

Bishop John stared with determination at his own reflection in the mirror. A sinister grin appeared on his face as his eyes held a piercing red gleam.

Claire Hollis, Ph.D.

Deceived

7

The sun shone brightly down upon the exclusive golf and country club, and a gentle breeze blew through the trees creating the perfect environment for a great game of golf. Prime Minister Catlin stood alone by his golf cart sipping on his chilled bottle of spring water. He was taking a moment out of this very important game to re-gather his thoughts and to concentrate on his strategies.

His opponent was King Ahmad, and Prime Minister Catlin desperately wanted to beat him. King Ahmad had known that Prime Minister Catlin was not much of a golfer, and that was why the King had suggested the game. The rivalry between their two nations had been going on for centuries, and it overflowed onto the golf course.

Suddenly, he sensed the presence of someone or something behind him.

Prime Minister Catlin turned to find a smartly dressed petite woman standing there, wearing an expensive, black suit. Her long black hair was neatly groomed into a barrette, exposing a pair of exquisite diamond earrings. She was a very attractive woman, and the Prime Minister was taken back with surprise.

Trying to open his mouth to speak, the Prime Minister found that he could not for his lips were stuck together. Puzzled at the present scenario, he looked at Lana, perplexed.

"Prime Minister, would you like to win this game?" She smiled sweetly at him.

Uncertain as to why his lips were stuck together preventing him from speaking, the Prime Minister could only nod to her.

Lana continued to grin. "I thought so. You can have what you desire," she assured him. "We will talk when you are finished. Go directly to your room after the game, and I will meet you there."

She turned and walked behind a tree, vanishing just as quickly as she had come. Now, the Prime Minister was even more confused. Who was this woman, and how could she give him the ability to win the game? He hurried over to his awaiting group of companions.

There were nine holes left to play. King Ahmad was waiting for Catlin.

"What took you so long?" The King pestered him. "You aren't trying to get out of losing are you?" Catlin realized that no one had see Lana.

As they approached the next hole, Catlin was overcome with an incredible sense of confidence. Feeling like he had the ability of a champion, he strode up to the tee with an air of certainty. Not sure of its source, he snickered to himself. "Either I am incredibly vain," he thought, "or I am just pretending to be a great golfer, because I know that I certainly am not!"

Catlin focused for a minute and then took a swing. The ball flew high in the air, plopped down around ten feet away from the hole, and rolled directly into the pocket. Catlin threw his arms in the air in great surprise while King Ahmad cried out, "Lucky shot!"

They joked at Catlin's sudden success; however, when the same scenario continued to repeat itself for the rest of the game, King Ahmad began to get upset.

It was not a game of skill and talent anymore. It seemed as though some magnetic force was pulling Catlin's golf ball right into the hole every time.

"I don't know what you have done, or how you did it, but this is impossible!" King Ahmad said angrily. One could almost see sparks fly as he spoke, he was so mad.

Unable to hide back a smile, Catlin reminded the King, "This golf game, and this particular golf course was your idea." At that, King Ahmad stormed off of the green, throwing his club off into the shrubbery.

Prime Minister Catlin chuckled to himself as his driver opened the limo door for him. As he settled into his seat, he meditated on the unexpected victory of today's golf game. He certainly had not anticipated this outcome, for sure. He also thought about the strange woman he had met and wondered if the pretty little lady truly would be meeting him back at his room. He smiled to himself and thought, "I sure would like to see her again."

He opened the door to his presidential suite. There she was, sitting politely on the rose colored couch placed next to the picturesque window that overlooked a lake. Beside her, on a cherry wood end table sat a beautiful bouquet of fresh flowers. An elegant array of hors d'oeuvres was spread out on the coffee table in front of her, accompanied by a shiny silver tea set.

"Now, this is what I call heaven!" He thought to himself.

"Hello, Catlin!" Lana greeted him warmly. She patted the velvet couch. "Please, come and join me."

Catlin closed the door behind him, and walked over to the couch, as if in a trance. He had somewhat expected her to be here-had *hoped* she would be here-yet, was still in shock that she actually *was* here. He slowly sat down beside her.

"I have some very good news for you, Catlin." She reached over and placed her hand on his arm quickly sending electric shocks through him. He glanced sharply at her hand. Where is this power coming from? He could not help but wonder.

Noticing his response, Lana continued on, "Since childhood, it has been your dream to rule the world, and have everyone esteem you highly. Well…" She gently squeezed his arm. "I am here to inform you that your dream is coming true. You will soon rule the world, and have the unlimited powers that you have always dreamed of. This King that you played golf with today will be kissing your feet, and begging you for mercy. How would you like that, Catlin?"

"I'm, uuhh, I, hmm..." Catlin stammered. He couldn't even think straight enough to respond. He cleared his throat again.

"Today is the last day that you will ever be speechless," she reassured him. "After today, you will deliver speeches that will capture the hearts of millions around the world; all will adore you.

"I will meet you again tomorrow evening in Paris for dinner," Lana instructed. "You will be contacted tomorrow about your transportation, as you will be traveling in one of our private jets."

"By the way, my name is Lana." She quickly stood up and disappeared.

Catlin sat there in a daze. He was so mesmerized by her presence that he was not even sure how she left the room, or when. He knew that she was not what she appeared to be, and that she was of the demonic world, but he didn't care. He was familiar with the kingdom of darkness, and was not intimidated; to the contrary, he was actually drawn to it.

He reached over and touched his arm. His skin still tingled from her touch, and the scent of her perfume still lingered in the air. Had it been a dream, or was the pretty lady actually here?

Catlin focused his thoughts back to her words, and on what she had said. Lana had declared that he would rule the world. She was right, that had been his lifelong dream. He would do *anything* for fame and fortune. Why, he even had his own father assassinated in order to get his position. Would he actually become the ruler of the world? For some reason, he believed her. Was it because he had won today's golf game, or was there some other unseen power that was causing him to follow her?

"I guess I'll find out tomorrow," Catlin thought as he leaned back on the couch and closed his eyes. He unconsciously shivered as a chilly draft blew over him.

Deceived

8

At exactly eight o'clock the following evening, Catlin sat at a small round table covered by a white linen tablecloth and a glowing candle. The table was set with enough fine china for three guests, and three golden goblets sat waiting to be filled. Catlin had been flown in on a private jet and escorted to this remote conference facility by some officials that Lana had sent to him earlier in the day. Now, he was waiting for her arrival.

Precisely one minute later, the door swiftly opened and Lana entered the room. Following closely behind her was a towering man, well over six feet tall. He had the build of a football player with features that could have graced the cover of any magazine.

Lana led him over to Catlin, who immediately stood to greet them.

"Catlin, I want you to meet Bishop John," Lana introduced. "Bishop John, meet Prime Minister Catlin."

The two men instinctively shook each other's hand. It was explosive! There was a web of lightning that flashed between them when their hands touched. An immediate bonding took place as they nodded to one another.

Each man eyed the other carefully, wondering why Lana had chosen him. Bishop John guessed that Catlin was probably somewhere in his thirties, like himself' and he couldn't help but notice how perfectly dressed he was.

Catlin had heard of Bishop John, although he had never met him. Catlin knew that he was a gifted orator, and could capture any audience. He was full of charisma, and his appearance was very holy. "This should be fun," Catlin thought to himself as they both assisted Lana as she sat down at the table.

Upon being seated, Lana burst with pride at the two men surrounding her. They were both extremely handsome, charming and intelligent. Bishop John had short blond hair and captivating baby-blue eyes, while Prime Minister Catlin was blessed with beautiful olive skin, dark eyes, and dark hair which he wore shoulder length. His square jaw line was tight as if he were biting down on something. Yes, these two men were the perfect candidates for the master plan, and Lana was very pleased.

She snapped her fingers at the two servers standing at attention against the wall. They immediately came forward and took the drink orders of the three guests. The meeting was being held at a small resort in Paris and Lana had reserved the entire facility to insure complete privacy. Her council provided the servers so that no information could leak to the outside world. Lana had demanded complete confidentiality.

Lana smiled at the two men. "I am so glad to see that you two like each other, because very soon, you will be inseparable," she said sweetly. "We will discuss the fate of planet earth over dinner."

Small talk continued as a basket of fresh rolls was brought to the table and passed around. A light salad and hot soup was then served, followed by the main course. After the last tidbit of filet was swallowed, and the dishes were cleared, Lana put down her napkin and said, "Now, let's get down to business.

"It's time to control the earth. Mankind is doing a miserable job, and it is time to do something about it," She said as she reached over and grabbed each man by the hand. "That's why you're here. Together, we are going to solve the problems of mankind, and together we are going to change the world." She smiled at both of them, as they also grinned at one another. An undercurrent of greed and manipulation flowed between them.

Lana let go of their hands as she continued, "In order to obtain control of the earth, a major catastrophe needs to occur that would cause people to panic, to think that there is no hope in sight. Just when it would seem that everything is hopeless, Prime Minister Catlin, you will appear on the scene and bring peace and safety to the world."

Catlin and Bishop John continued to listen with expectancy as Lana unfolded her plan.

"Originally, my plan was to create a system failure within the world's computer network; but then people would simply go back to living the same way they did before computers, and that's not catastrophic enough.

"So, I've decided to have a nuclear bomb explode that will shake the earth so violently that some of the nuclear plants will have a melt down and wipe out many people, creating worldwide chaos. There will be so much radiation released that everyone will be affected," Lana paused as a server brought them dishes of chocolate mousse and hot cups of coffee. She took a sip before she continued.

"Now, here is the good part," she said. "Just when the world thinks that life is over and there isn't any way anyone can survive the radiation, Bishop John will perform the greatest miracle ever and will save the earth."

Bishop John looked at Lana, astonished. "How can I save the world?" He asked.

Lana grabbed his arm. "This will be on international TV," she explained. "You will declare that God has given you the power to save the earth if man will just follow you. Then you will step outside and blow into the air. We will cause the radiation to leave the atmosphere, making it appear as though you blew it away. All of the inhabitants of the earth will fall at your feet because they will owe their lives to you.

"Bishop John, you will begin your miracles tomorrow. You will be known around the world within a week. You will be on every TV station and people will be totally amazed at your signs and wonders. Remember, it is our leader, Satan, who is supplying you with this power." She looked at him, awaiting his response.

Bishop John sat up taller as Lana spoke; pride had now completely taken control. A sinister smile appeared on his face, and his eyes took on a red glow. "Yes," he thought to himself, "This is a good plan; this is a good plan, indeed."

He excitedly put his hand on Lana's shoulder and said, "Please tell me more."

Lana laughed at his response; this was entirely too easy. These two humans were so selfish and full of greed, that she had them completely wrapped around her little finger. They would be willing to do *anything* she said.

"Okay," Lana continued. "This is where Catlin comes in." She turned to the Prime Minister who sat up straight in his chair. He could hardly wait to hear what his role would be in this magnificent plot.

"After you two officially meet publicly, you will become best friends, and Bishop John will always be pointing everyone to you," Lana instructed and both men nodded their approval. "Always be seen together in public and become very visible to the world. From that point on, Bishop John will only be able to perform miracles when he is in your presence. Until then, we will make sure that he accomplishes enough miracles to get the world's attention. He will then recommend that you become the leader of the world, and naturally everyone will agree. They will all love you both so much by then, that they will be willing to do anything you say.

"After you gain complete control, you will establish a one-world government with one monetary system," Lana ordered. "You are not to let anyone, and I mean anyone, get close to you except for Bishop John and myself."

Lana glanced at Catlin. "We have arranged for your wife to go on an extended vacation. You are not to tell her anything," she warned. "We will see to it that she is entertained enough to stay out of the way."

These men had no clue as to what they were *really* getting into; they were so wrapped up into their own greed and selfish desires, they didn't really care.

"Now, to the crucial part," Lana spoke on. "After this has all been set up, I want you to stamp out each and every follower of Jesus Christ. I don't want any 'believer' to be left alive."

She looked at them both closely. They looked back at her with puzzled looks. Prime Minister Catlin shook his head in doubt, and questioned, "How are we supposed to do that?"

"Easy! They are all believers of the Bible, and it states that there will someday be a man in control who will establish a law that states that no one can buy or sell without a mark on their forehead or hand. They are expecting it, and therefore, they won't do it. How much easier can this be? All you have to do is make it a law, and then kill all of those who refuse to accept the mark.

"This is the plan," Lana explained."I want you to start right away getting this set in motion. Register every human on the earth by taking a picture of the iris of their eye. Once you have done that, the rest is easy.

"We have created a computer chip that is so tiny it will fit into the blood stream. It can detect any physical problems within the human body, and can't even be seen by the human eye.

"It's this same chip that you are to stamp into their hand or forehead: it's so small that it will go under the skin's surface without them feeling a thing.

"Computers can detect it. The mark will be 'www' which translates into 'six, six, six', and the image of their iris. This image, plus 'www', will become the identification that will be embedded into their skin. It will become a law that no one will be able to buy or sell without this mark. By the time the mark is established, the entire world will be on the same monetary system.

"The 'real' believers will *never* agree to let the computer chip be placed on their hand or forehead. They know that the Bible teaches that if they take the mark, then they will never have another chance with God. Their fate would be doomed and forever sealed for an eternity without Him.

"Kill everyone who doesn't have a chip. Convince the world that they are doing Bishop John a favor by getting rid of all of his enemies who refuse to worship him."

Lana squinted her eyes at them, and lowered her voice, slowly emphasizing each word clearly, "I need you to rid the world of all of the Christians. Track them down. Infiltrate their meetings and plant tracking devices on them so that we will know where they are, at all times. There are certain things we cannot do because they have God's guardian angels surrounding and protecting them, but we can put devices on them to track and arrest them. Then..." She paused to accentuate her point, "we kill them!"

Bishop John and Catlin looked at each other in complete agreement, as they licked their lips and wondered what the blood of the enemy would taste like. Lana stood up as they finished their meal, and proposed a toast.

"This is a historical moment in time, history, and in all eternity," she said. "You two are about to meet your leader, face to face."

Satan himself suddenly appeared before them, and they fell to the floor, prostrate in reverence. He commanded them to rise and take their seats. There was complete silence before Satan finally spoke.

"Lana, you have chosen well; I commend you," he said before turning to the two men. "You two can have anything you want; wealth, women, drugs, power, popularity, anything. You name it, and it is yours. Very soon, you two will rule the world."

Although the two men were terrified at his appearance and could not look at Satan directly in the face, they did sneak side glances at him. On his face was a mischievous evil grin, and his eyes shot forth sparkles of excitement. Satan was undoubtedly happy. He had been preparing for centuries for this day.

Satan suddenly turned to Lana. His threatening gaze frightened her as he barked, "See to it that everyone worships them, and kill those who don't!"

With that said, Satan vanished from the room.

Claire Hollis, Ph.D.

Deceived

9

People all over the world were embracing Christianity. People had so much love that their priority in life was to share the Word of God, help those who were less fortunate, and fellowship together. The Word of God was being taught in the workplace, in homes, in schools, and in the community. Bible studies were occurring during lunch breaks; students would gather for prayer before and after school sessions. Homemakers would arise early to study and read the Bible before their families got up. People would pray for one another on elevators and on buses.

All were in a hurry to get done what they *had* to do so that they could have extra time for the things of God. Miracles, healings, and deliverances were common. God was convicting people of their sins and drawing people to himself in great multitudes.

JJ and Lynn were busy teaching new converts how to get rid of any demonic activity in their lives through the Word of God, and how to keep it out. Christians were learning to discern what was of God, and what was of the devil.

The humans that the demons had control of began to infiltrate the Christian meetings. They were very subtle at first pretending to accept Jesus as their Lord and Savior. They would volunteer for everything, and give huge offerings. These humans would be so sweet, wonderful, and helpful that they would work themselves into a position of respect, authority, and leadership. They had the most religious sounding prayers, and they knew all of the right things to say. They could counterfeit all of the miracles and healings that were taking place. Because they looked like Christians, they were able to deceive many. Eventually, they would try to divide the group through criticism and gossip. The demons who were working through these people were experts at what they were doing.

JJ and Lynn were at home one evening when they received a disturbing phone call from a pastor friend of theirs who was experiencing this problem in his church, which was divided and was about to split apart. Pastor Joshua had called JJ in desperation because he needed immediate help. JJ suggested that he and Pastor Joshua meet with Kyle, the young man who was causing all of the problems.

Kyle had been secretly assigned by Lana's group to destroy Pastor Joshua's church. He had developed his own little following, and had convinced them that they were right, and all the others were wrong. They had planned to leave together to start their own group.

A meeting was scheduled with Kyle for the next afternoon at the church. JJ and Pastor Joshua arrived early to discuss the situation and to pray. At the appointed time, Kyle arrived at the church. The secretary led Kyle into the Pastor's office, and Pastor Joshua introduced the men before they all sat down. JJ noted that Kyle was a nice looking guy with a clean-cut appearance. His sandy blonde hair and mustache was neatly groomed, and it appeared that he worked out in the gym. Kyle's facial expression was hard and his teeth were clenched. It was obvious that he was not overjoyed at this meeting.

He began to murmur under his breath about being falsely accused of causing division, and throwing his spiritual weight around when JJ cut him off.

"Kyle," JJ said. "The Lord has just revealed to me who you are and why you are here."

Kyle glared at him, puzzled and in disbelief. His eyes squinted, as they fixed on JJ as if to hypnotize him.

"You are on the wrong team," JJ ignored Kyle's glare. "Satan and his kingdom loses, and God's team wins. Why would you want to be a part of a losing team?"

He just kept staring at JJ.

"It doesn't matter what you have done," JJ continued, "God loves you so much that He sent His son to die for you in order that you might live with Him for eternity. Satan will spend his eternity in a lake of fire."

Kyle continued to stare at JJ. His expression remained frozen.

"You can get rid of all of the demonic spirits that are controlling you right now," JJ urged. "You can be free!"

Kyle still didn't move. His eyes remained fixed on JJ when suddenly he dropped his head in his hands as a flood of tears burst forth.

JJ leaned forward and placed his hand on Kyle's shoulder. "In the name of Jesus, I bind up every evil spirit that is in Kyle," JJ commanded. "You cannot hinder him from accepting Jesus Christ as his Lord and Savior."

Kyle stopped crying and looked up at JJ. His face was no longer hateful and tightly drawn; instead, it was replaced with a timid look. "You don't understand," he said. "If I accept Jesus into my life, then they will kill me and my wife."

"Kyle, they can kill the body, but God's Word says not to fear those who can kill the body because they can't touch your soul. Instead, fear God, because He is the one who is able to destroy both your soul *and* your body in hell."

Kyle sat thinking for a few minutes. "If I do this, would you be willing to come to my home and pray that my wife, Cindy, will also accept Jesus?"

"Sure, we can go as soon as we finish here."

Kyle sat upright in his chair. He closed his eyes and said, "God, I believe you're there. This is Kyle Johnson speaking to you. I've been on Satan's team since I was a little boy, and now I want to switch sides. I've made a mess of my life trying to do things my way; but now I want to give you control of my life. I want to accept what your son, Jesus, did when he died on the cross in order that I can be forgiven of my sins, and live with you for eternity."

He opened his eyes and saw a beam of light come into the room, quickly disappearing into him. He also saw and heard a host of God's angels singing and making merry over his decision. Kyle didn't understand what he was seeing, but this was a symbol of God's Holy Spirit who comes into every believer when they accept Jesus.

JJ immediately began to command all of the demon spirits to leave Kyle, who had the ability to see things in the supernatural realm. He later told JJ that as he would call out a demon, Kyle could see it leave. He told JJ that they were small and black, and that he saw God's angels swiftly taking them away.

JJ then prayed that God would give Kyle love, peace, joy, happiness, a sound mind, boldness, purity, good health, prosperity, and all of the blessings that God had to offer.

Kyle was a new man. When they were all finished, he told them that he felt as light as a feather. He exclaimed, "It feels so great to get rid of all of the excess baggage!"

All three of them left in Pastor Joshua's car to go see Kyle's wife. During the drive across town, Kyle informed them how the occult world was meeting regularly and assigning their members to infiltrate different churches.

"It's a gigantic system," he explained. "There's not a Christian group anywhere on the planet that does not have a counterfeit in its midst."

They pulled up in the driveway of a quaint little cottage. Cindy was stooped down in the front yard over some flowers. She was wearing a big brimmed hat and garden gloves on her hands to protect her from the thorns of the rose bush that she was pruning. Upon hearing the car in the driveway, she stood to greet them. Her face revealed that she was surprised to see Pastor Joshua.

Kyle was beaming. He rushed over to Cindy, put his arm around her, and led her over to JJ and Pastor who had gathered outside of the car. He quickly introduced Cindy and JJ before inviting them all into the house.

"Honey, I have some good news to tell you," Kyle shared excitedly.

Cindy wrinkled her brows at him, perplexed by his strange behavior. "Okay…" she replied as they stepped into the house.

Two hours later, Pastor Joshua and JJ emerged from the house joyfully because Cindy had also received Jesus as the Lord of her life. They prayed that God's angels would protect Kyle and Cindy as they drove away.

Deceived

10

Monday morning rolled around as folks began to prepare for another workweek. Lana had done the legwork for Bishop John to debut on network television. He was scheduled for a live interview on one of highest rated news programs in the country. Tim Blake was the most respected and most received reporters known, so it was a high honor for Bishop John to appear on Blake's program. The revival fires were spreading so quickly throughout America that Christianity had become a "hot" topic for the media.

Bishop John and Tim were seated comfortably on the set waiting to begin the interview. The "record" light came on, and Tim immediately began. Much to Tim's dismay, however, Bishop John suddenly stood up and pointed to the producer who was seated in a wheelchair behind one of the cameras.

"Rise up and walk!" He yelled.

Tim stopped speaking and stared at Bishop John. One of the cameraman zoomed in on Bishop John while another man focused his camera on the producer.

"Whaaat?..."Tim turned to Bishop John.

"I said, 'Rise up and walk!" Bishop John repeated while pointing to the producer, Martin Bailey, who sat red-faced as his jaw dropped open in disbelief. He could not believe that this was happening on live television before millions of viewers.

Bishop John marched over to Martin, and waved his hands up in the air. "You can walk," he exclaimed. "Now do it!"

Martin looked at the folks around him who were as shocked as he was. Born with a disabling disease that weakens the muscles, Martin had never walked a day in his life. He looked back up at Bishop John who waved his hands up again in the air.

Martin placed his hands on the sides of the wheelchair and hesitantly pushed his way up. Everyone gasped in total astonishment as Martin planted his feet solidly on the ground, straightened his legs, and pushed himself upright into a standing position. He reached out and grabbed Bishop John's hands who helped to steady him. Martin slowly bent his knees and crouched down. He then stood back up to see if his muscles were really working. He held on to Bishop John's hands and repeated the bending exercises several more times. Convinced that he truly had been healed, Martin let go of Bishop John. Gasps could be heard throughout the studio as Martin stood on his own for the first time in his entire life.

Tim Blake stood frozen in place, completely dismayed. Never before in all of his years as a journalist had he ever witnessed anything like this. He had known Martin for over twenty years, and this was truly a miracle.

Suddenly someone shouted exuberantly from the studio audience. A loud cheer arose as Martin stepped forward and gave Bishop John a hug.

"It's a miracle! It's a miracle!" He cried. "I can't believe this just happened. It is truly a miracle!"

To add to the wonder of it all, a big ball of light suddenly entered into the room and floated between Bishop John and Martin. A beautiful angel suspended in the air appeared within the light. He outstretched his wings behind them. Smiling, he declared, "Bishop John has been approved by God, and has been sent to lead the world into unity. He will lead you in the way that you should go, follow him." As quickly as he appeared, the angel then disappeared.

The cameramen were scurrying to get the best footage of this wondrous turn of events. Tim Blake's professionalism kicked in as he regained his composure and stepped up to the camera to recap what had just happened. Completing his summary of this breaking news story, Tim moved on to a commercial break reassuring viewers that they would "be right back!"

Immediately the phones began to ring off of the hook. Reporters were everywhere, and there was general pandemonium throughout the entire studio. The ratings for the show skyrocketed; and before the day was over, the Tim Blake Show was being repeated on every news channel around the world.

The camera crew had caught every bit of the live drama on tape, including the angel's visitation. Lana had to manipulate some images in order to do that, since angels—good or bad—don't usually show up on cameras. She had worked very hard on preparing special clothing in order to pull that off. But, she had done it, it had worked, and now, the angel's instructions were being broadcast all over the world.

Bishop John became an instant leader. Even the real miracles that were taking place among the Christian community were no match for this angelic appearance that Lana had set up. No one had ever seen anything like this before.

Within a week, many of the new converts, who didn't have much knowledge of the Bible, had their eyes fixed on Bishop John. The older, more mature Christians continued to watch from a distance, speculating on his authenticity.

Meanwhile, Lana remained very busy. She was full of devilish ideas, and she had the "man" power to carry them out.

Deceived

11

There were a lot of wars; one nation against another. Lana had arranged for a meeting between two border countries that were constantly fighting. They were always in the news, and the people of the world were very uneasy as one of the countries bragged about having a nuclear bomb.

It was a miracle just to get them to sit down at the same table together, but Lana had arranged it. She made sure that all of the top world leaders were there, including Prime Minister Catlin. Tim Blake was the journalist chosen to cover this worldwide event.

Everyone was seated in the room with their interpreter's headphones on, so the meeting began. Lana was present, disguised as a press reporter. There was a gleam in her jet black eyes.

The two leaders began their negotiations, and it was obvious that they were getting nowhere fast. Rage could be seen on both of their faces as the bickering went back and forth.

Unexpectedly, some mysterious beings wearing black pants, shirts, and shoes appeared within the room. They had long, black hair, and their faces were white with special make-up that Lana had prepared for their faces and hands.

The security guards immediately drew their weapons and aimed them at the intruders. The leaders all stopped talking and stared at the new visitors in irritation. Lana had one of her comrades positioned as a cameraman to catch everything on tape.

One of the visitors held his hand up to the security guards causing them to become frozen in their tracks, unable to move. Another one of the beings walked up to where the two world leaders sat.

"Both of you will be dead within the hour, and your countries will be totally annihilated. There will be nothing left, only sand and dirt will cover the area," he growled at them. "It has already begun." He pointed to a cabinet against the wall. "Turn on the television set and you will see what I mean."

The two leaders glanced at each other, perplexed. One of them nodded to a young man who was standing near the cabinet and directed him to open it up, and turn the TV on. The young man quickly obeyed.

The entire room watched in silence as the news report came on. The breaking story was of a huge tornado that had formed off the coast, although it remained stationary at the moment. It was a phenomenon that meteorologists couldn't explain because there weren't any weather conditions to attribute to it; and, it wasn't going anywhere. It was hazy-red in color and the largest tornado ever recorded. The magnitude of its size was so enormous that even the veteran weathermen were afraid, and, it was very unnatural for it to be just sitting there, as though waiting for something.

All eyes turned back to the mysterious figure in the center of the room. He pointed to the two leaders at the table. Before anyone could say a word, however, Prime Minister Catlin jumped up from his chair, and boldly approached the men.

"I don't know who you are, how you got here, or what you are planning, but I have a proposition for you," Catlin directed to the mysterious figure. "These two men have been enemies for a very long time now, with no reconciliation in sight. If they would agree to live in peace and harmony with no more fighting, would you consider changing your plans?"

The man in black looked at Prime Minister Catlin for a moment, considering his proposal. Nodding, he then directed his gaze at the two world leaders and told them that he would give them five minutes to make some negotiations. Everyone in the room sat nervous and spellbound.

At the threat of total annihilation, they were suddenly able to agree on the negotiations, and began to make each other offers.

At this extended show of mercy, the two leaders smiled at one another, and shook hands vibrantly. In order to seal the pact, they decided to unite one of their sons and one of the other's daughter in matrimony. Instead of fighting over the borders, they agreed to come together and form one nation. The two men stood and embraced before turning to the audience. Everyone cheered.

The room quieted down as the man in black turned to address Prime Minister Catlin, "You have done a good thing here today. Because of you, I have changed my mind and will not destroy these men or their nations." With that, the mysterious figures disappeared, and the security guards were able to move about freely again.

The news reporter could be heard from the television: *...No, there is nothing wrong with the camera, Bill, the tornado has simply disappeared! It is nowhere in sight. This is a phenomenon that cannot be explained. As you can see, the weather conditions have returned to normal, and the sun is shining brightly. Now, back to you, Bill...*

The young man clicked off the television set as Prime Minister Catlin took control of the rest of the meeting. Lana sat in her seat with a cynical smile on her face. Everything had come off very smoothly, and was falling into place. She could hardly contain her excitement.

"Today has been a very successful day for me," she thought to herself. "Satan is going to be so proud of me. Someday soon, I will be ruling with him! I am such a genius!" She snickered to herself.

The sounds of clapping jolted Lana's thoughts back to the present. Everyone was applauding Catlin for his successful intervention of a potential catastrophe.

Lana suddenly jumped up and shouted, "Cat-lin!...Cat-lin!...Cat-lin!..."

Soon, the entire room was on their feet joining in, "Cat-lin!...Cat-lin!...Cat-lin!..." It sounded like a group of cheerleaders at a sporting event.

Prime Minister Catlin stood before them, as a surge of power flooded his being.

Claire Hollis, Ph.D.

Deceived

12

The media went wild trying to gather as much information as they could regarding Prime Minister Catlin and Bishop John. Every major news outlet was in competition for the best coverage. The world's largest magazine could not decide which one to place on their cover first, so they profiled both men simultaneously. Lana read the issue, and began to laugh hysterically. The world was already putting them together, and she didn't even have to arrange it!

Lana's strategy was for Bishop John to demonstrate many more miracles over the next few months, and for Prime Minister Catlin to settle more peace talks and intervene in war outbreaks. She wanted them to be established as worldwide heroes before she put them together.

During this time, the mature Christians around the world were continuing to instruct and teach the new converts the Word of God. Only a small percentage were qualified to teach and preach in comparison to the large number of people who were eager to hear and to be taught. Lana assigned some of her officers to infiltrate as Christian leaders and teachers.

Meanwhile, JJ and Lynn's book, *This Means War*, continued to soar on the bestsellers list, second in sales only to the Holy Bible. There wasn't anything that Lana and her group could do to stop it. They had tried, but mighty angels of God were guarding every aspect of the book, preventing them from attack. *This Means War* was being read over and over again by individuals all over the world, and people were gaining knowledge of spiritual warfare.

The two spiritual sides were becoming more obvious as the human population was being split down the middle. It was as though there was an imaginary line drawn, and everyone was on one side or the other; either one was a believer, loved God, and accepted the sacrifice that Jesus Christ had made for mankind, or one was on the devil's side.

Because of the large number of counterfeits that Lana had placed within the Christian groups, it appeared as though the majority of the human race was on the Lord's side.

Deceived

13

Prime Minister Catlin continued to gain world-wide attention. He truly had to be the greatest con artist that ever existed for people really loved him. His extremely good looks captured the eyes of females everywhere, and his charismatic spirit won the respect of all men. People were always surrounding him, trying to capture his attention; and Catlin would always smile and wave at everyone as though they were his best friends. The people loved him and were drawn to his magnetic personality.

Prime Minister Catlin's greatest strength, however, was in the area of peacekeeping. He knew that this "gift" came from Lana and her demonic power. Because he had gained the respect of all nations, world leaders were willing to listen to him, and to heed his advice.

He had the ability to walk into a tumultuous situation and calm the storm. Catlin was able to break beyond language and cultural barriers in a way that no man had ever been able to do before.

Because of Catlin's efforts, the world's trade system was flowing very smoothly, allowing the superpowers to enjoy great prosperity. The world's wealth was at an all-time high and Prime Minister Catlin was revered as a god.

Bishop John was also enjoying international attention and popularity. Because of the great revivals that had been forthcoming from all over the world, "religion" had captured the attention of the media. And, because Bishop John had been performing miracles everywhere, people continued to gaze at him in complete reverence.

Although Bishop John towered in height over the majority of those around him, his character was soft and gentle. He always wore a white robe as a symbol of purity, and was ready to embrace whoever came to him in need. Because he was so conciliatory, all religious denominations acknowledged Bishop John as their spiritual leader; and many of the top spiritual leaders would often seek his guidance and counsel. Most believed that God's favor rested upon him.

There was, however, a small number of mature Christians who had discerned that something was not quite right about Bishop John. They were very well aware of what the Bible predicted would happen in the "end times" and were not deceived. That was a slight concern to Lana. In order for their plans to succeed, she needed to deceive as many as possible. But that was not something she would worry about just yet. Lana was currently waiting for the right moment to put the Prime Minister and the Bishop together.

Lana smiled to herself as the master plan continued to unfold.

Claire Hollis, Ph.D.

Deceived

14

L ana made her appearance at the entrance of
Satan's headquarters. The two henchmen that
usually escorted her into his quarters stepped
forward to take her by the arms. Not this time! Lana
roughly threw her arms out, flinging the henchmen
against the wall. She haughtily marched forward in
determination.

Two large gates stood before the heavy door
to Satan's headquarters. The doors were made of
something that even the demons could not penetrate;
and they would not dare to even if they could. Each
gate had a big, brass knocker in the middle with
Satan's image on it.

Lana stopped abruptly. She knew that no one ever opened these gates without first knocking and being admitted. Only one person had ever done that. It was Jesus Christ himself. Lana's mind instantly shifted back to that day as she reached for the brass knocker.

The entire demonic kingdom had gathered for the biggest celebration party of all times. The lower class demons were gathered on the outside while Lana and her group convened inside of Satan's headquarters. Everyone was so excited because they had won. It was a victory celebration! They were laughing and jeering at how awful Jesus had looked as he hung bloody and beaten on the cross. They excitedly recalled how Christ's joints were out of place, and how he was so thirsty. Many of the demons were rolling on the floor because they were so hysterical. Their laughter could be heard throughout the universe. Yes, Lana could remember it all as if it had just happened yesterday.

Lana shivered as she recalled what happened next. She remembered noticing in the back of her mind how it had suddenly grown quiet in the outer courts, although they were so drunk with their own hysteria that they gave no attention to the outside party. They had won the big one. They had killed Him (so they thought!) Satan and his officials continued to celebrate.

One of the little demons told her later that they were out there celebrating when they noticed a figure surrounded by a bright light approaching them. He walked steadily toward their camp with a look of authority on His face.

The party was instantly over for they immediately recognized the glowing figure as being Jesus Christ.

They all knew Him, and He knew everyone, because He had created them to begin with. At one time, they all lived together with God Almighty in Heaven. They were not strangers.

All of the lower class demons cowered in fear, making a path for Him, giving Him plenty of room. They became paralyzed in total disbelief. They thought they had killed Him! What was He doing here alive? They were completely silent, although they could still hear the cheers, squealing, and laughter coming from the main headquarters.

Jesus calmly walked through the path they made and up to the gate, swung it open, and stepped up to the big door. It was obvious that He was on assignment because He did not even bother to open the door; he just walked right through it.

Satan, along with the thirteen, was sitting at the long black table. They were all drunk with the excitement of their victory. The room was dimly lit, and there was a stench in the air.

Suddenly, the headquarters filled up with a great light. Everyone immediately shielded their eyes with their hands as Jesus Christ entered into the room. As the blinding light cast away all of the darkness, everyone, including Lana, shrieked back in complete fear. Everyone, that is, except Satan. He sat frozen in his chair as he stared totally aghast at Jesus.

Not a sound was heard as all eyes were on the King of Kings, and the Lord of Lords. Everyone trembled in terror.

Without saying a word, Jesus walked forward with all power and all authority toward Satan. Jesus and

Satan knew each other well. After all, Satan had once been the praise and worship leader in Heaven where they all had lived together, before God kicked him out. Jesus stopped before Satan, and stretched out His hand with His palm up. He simply said, "Keys, please!" Lana could recall seeing the nail prints in His hands.

Satan's eyes were still fixed in fear on Jesus as he reached over into a drawer under the table and pulled out two keys attached to a large ring. He had no choice but to obey. Satan's teeth clenched, and his eyes squinted as he relinquished the keys to Jesus.

Lana noticed that one key was imprinted with the word: *death*, while the other key said: *hell*.

Jesus turned and walked out of the room. The demons continued to silently shutter in horror as Sovereignty passed by. Jesus retraced His steps through the path of demons who had once known the glories of Heaven. He then disappeared.

The darkness immediately returned along with the pungent odor. Satan sat abased in his chair. He absolutely abhorred what had just happened. Mixed emotions of anger, humiliation, defeat, and fear welled up within him as he shouted, *"Jesus may have won this battle, but he hasn't won the war!"*

Satan stood and threw his hands up in the air, his face was overcome with rage as fire burned from his eyes. His voice distorted into a deep growl as he declared angrily, "You *will* stick with me as we find a way to overcome this obstacle. All of you made the right choice when you decided to follow me, and you gave me your allegiance. I'll prove to you that *I will* win the final battle! *I will* rule the world!"

Lana remembered that day all too well; that feeling of defeat and despair that she had experienced. Since they had all made their decision, there was no turning back. They had no other alternative but to follow Satan, and to go along with his plan.

There was no more partying that day. Instead, everyone was extremely distraught, wondering about what had just happened, and worrying about what was going to happen next. Out of fear, though, not a word was spoken as they kept their thoughts to themselves.

Claire Hollis, Ph.D.

Deceived

15

L ana's attention was immediately brought to the present as she folded her bony fingers over, making a fist to knock on the gate. "This is the day we've been waiting for. Satan will rule this planet, and I will be right by his side," she thought to herself.

Lana gently knocked on the door, received entrance, and bowed low as she entered. She waited in reverence until Satan released her to have a seat.

He immediately questioned her, "Lana, is your report a good one?"

"Yes, Master, it couldn't be better. Everything is in position, and I am putting our two men together next week.

"Give me six months, and I will have all of the earth's inhabitants identified so that our infiltrators can access any information necessary at any given time on anyone," Lana assured him confidently. "There will be one world leader with one world religion, and Bishop John and Prime Minister Catlin will be in complete control. We are in the process of developing one currency system for the world, as well."

Satan smiled his approval at her as she continued, "Right now, the world is operating in peace and prosperity. The new world religion is drowning out everything that is real, thanks to your ingenious plan to infiltrate their movement. We have counterfeited everything, and it is working."

Satan was very pleased at Lana's report. He abruptly frowned as he had a sudden thought, "Where are JJ and Lynn Murphy, and what are they doing?"

Lana was afraid that he was going to ask her that, so she was prepared with a lie. She knew that the new world order was not drowning out the revival of people coming to believe in Jesus Christ as their Savior and Lord. The counterfeits that she had placed among the Christians were deceiving some by their miracles, but they were not able to fool the ones who had Bible knowledge. Lana only told Satan what she knew he wanted to hear. He relied on her because he liked to keep a low profile and stay in his headquarters.

"In answer to your question, Master," Lana began, "JJ and Lynn are relaxing at home, not causing any problems."

Satan's eyes narrowed as he pierced her with a look. He snarled and small wafts of smoke came from his ears as he spoke. "If they're doing nothing, then something's up! They don't ever 'do nothing'! Don't you dare let those two out of your site for even a moment!" He warned angrily.

Calming down, Satan continued, "Lana, if you pull this off, I will reward you. Destroy all of the Christians, and unite the world with one political, religious, and monetary system, then you will receive your reward. I will make you ruler with me.

"I will enter into Prime Minister Catlin, and you will enter into Bishop John. Together, we will rule this world," Satan announced with a distorted growl. His eyes burned with flames as he waved his arms at her, "Now get busy! There is not a minute to spare!"

Lana bowed low as she backed out of the room. Just before she exited, she heard Satan hiss, "Don't let those two out of your site! I mean it, Lana. I *will not* have them messing up my plan!"

Claire Hollis, Ph.D.

Deceived

16

The appointed time to bring the two men together publicly had finally come. Lana had arranged for Prime Minister Catlin and Bishop John to come together as guests for a joint interview on Tim Blake's live television program. It was anticipated as being one of the highest rated shows ever, and the cost for commercial time skyrocketed.

Bishop John, Prime Minister Catlin, and Tim Blake met briefly in the green room before the interview. Both Catlin and Bishop John pretended that it was their first introduction. Tim then left to go open the program.

The first segment began as Tim engaged in some light talk before he dramatically announced, "Ladies and Gentlemen, I have a special treat for you.

"Tonight, the two most popular men in the world will meet for the first time ever, face to face," Tim paused, and stood up in anticipation, "Please welcome with me...Bishop John and Prime Minister Catlin!"

The two men walked out on to the stage as the studio audience immediately applauded. The second camera, operated by Matt Monroe, took over and zoomed in on their entrance. Matt was an infiltrator of Lana's and had been positioned at the station for many years.

Suddenly, a glorious rainbow appeared over Bishop John and Prime Minister Catlin, and showered little twinkles of light over them. Tim's mouth flew open, and for the second time on live television, he was at a loss for words. (The first time was during Bishop John's miracle performance.) Millions of viewers around the globe were glued to their screens.

The two men looked at each other triumphantly. Bishop John spoke, "God is pleased with our coming together; this rainbow is a sign of His approval. I believe that we are to work together. God has shown his approval of Prime Minister Catlin, and it is obvious that we should all follow him. He has brought peace to nations that were divided. Let us all *unite* in one accord to make this earth what God wanted it to be from the beginning. Let our motto be 'Peace.'"

Lana instantly appeared through the wall, and walked up to the two men encased in the rainbow. She had the appearance of a heavenly being adorned with special make-up in order to be seen by the camera. A bluish-white glow radiated from around her.

Tim continued to sit absolutely dumbfounded; never before witnessing anything so bizarre in his life.

Lana spoke to Prime Minister Catlin, "I have come from the throne of God to tell you that God wants you to be in charge of the earth. He will speak directly to you, and give you direction through Bishop John." Then she disappeared.

Both men were trying to appear calm, but on the inside they were both about to explode with excitement. Bishop John put his hands over his face, and appeared to be crying. He was actually laughing, but he didn't want anyone to know. He then fell forward to his knees, and knelt at his chair turning his head away from the camera. Everyone thought that he was sobbing although he was really laughing hysterically.

Catlin could not conceal his laughter either so he followed suit. Tim glanced around in disbelief at the two men kneeling at their seats, still not comprehending the reality of the situation. Finally, the two men regained composure and got back into their chairs. They looked over at Tim who was sitting speechless, as if in a trance.

Prime Minister Catlin took over the interview and turned to the camera. Matt zoomed in on him as he said, "I promise to be the best leader I can be for anyone who chooses to follow me. I will give up my life for you, if neccesary, for my objective is global peace." He brought his hand to his mouth and blew them a kiss. "I love you!"

The studio audience cheered; there was not a dry eye in the crowd. Television viewers were wiping away tears as well. JJ and Lynn were also watching, although they were not moved.

JJ turned to Lynn. "I'm not fooled by these men at all. How about you?"

"No, I'm not fooled, either. This is exactly what the Bible predicts. These two are the anti-Christ and the false prophet that will rule the world in the last seven years of time. Our work is cut out for us. We have to warn the Christians not to fall for these imposters."

JJ and Lynn were not the only ones who knew in their hearts that it was time for the end; thousands upon thousands of Christians around the world knew as well. Many others familiar with Bible prophecies were also aware of what was taking place.

They all knew of the false peace and the terrible wrath of God that would soon follow; they were all filled with excitement and anticipation of knowing that the time was short. They knew that it would not be long before they were to receive their final reward as promised in God's Holy Word.

Deceived

17

Over the next several months, Prime Minister Catlin achieved great success in settling conflicts and became known as the peacemaker, while Bishop John was referred to as God's chosen. The earth was at peace, except for one small area. It was considered a "hot spot", and it was thought that peace was impossible. Catlin had saved it for last because the tension was so serious.

One day, Prime Minister Catlin and Bishop John were both gathered in Catlin's office for business when Lana appeared. They both bowed in reverence before her. She told them to relax because she had a project that she needed them to take care of.

They both looked up, giving her their undivided attention. Lana looked absolutely striking in a beautiful red outfit, and seemed to be in an excellent mood.

She began by complimenting them on a job well done. Lana couldn't keep her eyes off of Bishop John, for she knew that one day soon, she was going to possess his body.

Her mind began to wander: *I like that body, so young and handsome. I am going to like living there and looking through those big blue eyes. I am sick of being so tiny; I can't wait to get into that six-foot frame. It will be fun to be a blond for a change.*

She shook her head. *Get a hold of yourself, Lana!*

Lana suddenly got serious, and addressed the men, "Men, I have some good news for you. Satan has been in complete control of the Middle East situation, and he has been keeping the hatred alive between Israel and the Arab nations for centuries. It was brother against brother, and mother against mother at first. And then, over the years, the conflict, hatred and jealousy has grown even stronger.

"Since both nations had the same father, they both feel like that land belongs to them. We are going to have all of the spirits that we have placed in the humans to suddenly become inactive so that there will be peace, and we want you..." Lana pointed her finger at the Prime Minister, "to get all of the credit."

The three of them gloated at one another. "Schedule a meeting with these nations and I will make sure that it will be televised. I will command all of the demon spirits in the people to 'back off' at exactly the same time allowing the nations to become friends." She then disappeared as quickly as she came.

Prime Minister Catlin and Bishop John sat and looked at each other. Before either of them could speak, the Prime Minister's secretary burst into the room, obviously quite shaken. She said, "Quick! Turn on the TV! There's a news bulletin saying that there's a meteorite that has gone off course and is headed straight for the earth! It's expected to hit tomorrow around four o'clock central standard time." She ran over and clicked the TV on.

Tim Blake could be heard saying: *We don't know where exactly, but it looks like it will hit somewhere in the Middle East. It isn't big enough to do much damage, but it could destroy as much as a city block. We have been told that it could possibly disintegrate before it hits. Again, I repeat, a meteorite has gone off course and is expected to hit the earth within the next twenty-four hours...*

Bishop John and the Prime Minister exchanged glances. How was this going to affect their most recent game plan?

All news outlets maintained live coverage with constant updates for the next twenty-four hours. Tim Blake was on the air for a large portion of the time, leaving only to catch a few hours of sleep. Everyone stayed fixed to their TV screens as they wondered what was going to happen. Just as predicted, the meteorite struck in the Middle East at 4:24pm. It hit the Dome of the Rock, the famous Muslim Temple in Jerusalem.

Tim Blake was in Israel shortly afterward with live footage of the damage: *I am here in Jerusalem witnessing the complete destruction of this building. The heat has just disintegrated the temple. The meteorite lost its strength on impact, and has disappeared, too. The area has been completely leveled.*

Small fires could be seen scattered around the vicinity. It was shocking to see the maze of underground passageways, rooms, and tunnels instantly exposed because of the meteorite. The area was roped off because of the potential danger of the tunnels collapsing.

The camera zoomed in on the damage as Tim reassured the viewers that the threat was over, and that this was the only destruction the world would experience.

Deceived

18

A meeting was scheduled between Bishop John, Prime Minister Catlin, and the leaders of the nations in conflict. Lana made sure that it was well advertised. Meanwhile, there was a powerful group of European nations that had formed a confederation uniting their countries under one political and monetary system. Their power came from their unity. They were in favor of the meeting, and were hoping that Prime Minister Catlin would succeed in bringing peace to the Middle East. This group of European leaders met to discuss the situation.

"If Prime Minister Catlin can bring peace to the Middle East, then I say we make him the President of our federation," one man suggested. Although he was not present at this particular meeting, Prime Minister

Catlin was a member of this group, and they all deeply respected him. He had won each member over with his charismatic personality.

"He'll never be successful," another man inserted. There was much discussion around the table.

"This is an impossible situation: they have never had peace."

"No, but the world loves the Prime Minister. If anyone can do it, he can."

"Hey!" One of the men piped up. "We already have a majority of the world's wealth in our control. If we make him the President, who knows? We may get it all!"

Another man muttered, "Yes, and if we *don't* make him the President, we will be in big trouble with the people!"

Many nodded their heads in agreement.

After much discussion, it was time to take a vote. Prime Minister Catlin was unanimously voted as the President of the Confederation. Because of Catlin's important meeting the next day with the leaders of the Middle East, it was decided to wait until afterward to announce their decision: absolutely no one was to know.

Tim Blake and the television crews were all assembled and in place the next day waiting for the meeting to begin. Lana had seen to it that cameraman Matt Monroe was there also, to catch everything on tape. It was being held in a building that overlooked where the Dome of Rock had been just a few days earlier.

The tension was felt between everyone, from the top officials down to the set-up crews and behind-the-scene workers.

The two leaders sat and stared at each other with hatred in their eyes, and one could immediately sense the strong enmity between them. As soon as the cameras started to roll, they each tried to cover it up with big smiles, although it was obvious to all that the hatred was there. And now, the Arabs were very upset because their most holy place had been destroyed.

The two men were already seated and posing for the camera when Prime Minister Catlin entered with Bishop John right beside him. Catlin bent over to the leaders and greeted them before sitting down in the middle.

Bishop John took the microphone and said, "Let us pray together to the god of our choice before we start this meeting." The two leaders eyed him curiously before they both consented.

Then Catlin asked them if they could join hands during the prayer as a gesture of oneness and unity. Hesitantly, they both agreed, because the live broadcast forced them to, not because they really wanted to. They were both aware of how honored and respected Prime Minister Catlin was around the world, and how important it was to agree with him.

Tim Blake could be heard off to the side, reporting: *...Prime Minister Catlin is doing it again! It's a miracle, folks! The meeting has just begun, and these two hostile leaders have already come into* *agreement on two things: first, by agreeing to pray together, and second, by joining hands in unity...*

As the Prime Minister made contact with their hands, every demonic spirit that had been causing division and trouble between them immediately became inactive. This was not only in the leaders, but it was also among the civilians as well. Lana had ordered that all spirits of division cease to operate.

All at once, a great commotion could be heard outside; so loud, in fact, that the men were unable to finish their prayer. Someone rushed to the window to see what the noise was. People were running rampant in the streets of Jerusalem. The city was filled with people who had assembled for today's meeting, but this was different. These people were running wild and screaming. They were running toward where the Dome of Rock had been.

Tim Blake was receiving a report through his earphones. He shouted out, "Someone turn on the TV. You won't believe what I am hearing!"

The TV in a nearby cabinet was flipped on. There were plenty of cameras in the area, as every nation had sent their TV crews there to cover the story about the meteorite and the meeting.

The picture on the TV screen showed an older man with a long white beard, panting and running from the uncovered maze of tunnels. Although the site had been blocked off and secured by guards because of the immediate danger of the ground collapsing, the old man had somehow managed to slip through and venture into one of the tunnels.

Perspiration was running down his face and dripping off the end of his nose. His cheeks were red and his voice was quivering. "It's there! It's in a room! I saw it. Oh my God, it's there!" He was shaking so severely that someone had to hold him up as he spoke. "The Ark of the Covenant, I saw it!"

With that declaration, gasps could be heard everywhere. People around the world were in shock. They could not believe it.

Upon hearing the news, the Israeli and the Arab leaders stood, laughing and shouting enthusiastically. Matt kept his camera directed at them every second, recording every moment on film.

After about an hour of excited dancing and praising, Prime Minister Catlin asked them all to please be seated. He stood in front of them and said, "Let's all share with each other, and live in peace and harmony together. I propose that we rebuild both of your temples. Let the Jewish people rebuild their temple here, and they can put the Ark of the Covenant in it like it was originally. The Dome of the Rock can be rebuilt a block away."

Catlin continued, "Let us also take down the borders between the two countries, and live as brothers. I will subsidize the entire amount and help with the building, in order that it can be done very quickly."

The two leaders nodded at Catlin in agreement, which seemed to satisfy them both. Without all of the demonic influence that had been a part of their lives, they were agreeable to almost anything. They truly wanted to live like brothers.

Lana loved it! As she observed from a close distance, she thought, "All I have to do is activate those demons again and we are right back where we started! I love this power. I think I will let them be friends for a while before I change the scene."

Israel was the central focus of every major network television station. The two top stories were the peace talks and the exposed opening left by the meteorite that disintegrated the Dome of the Rock.

As the news spread quickly, people emptied out of their homes and into the streets of Jerusalem to celebrate. They gathered by the multitudes around the opening, joined hands, and danced in big circles around the location. Jews and Arabs were holding hands, and every other circle was going around in a different direction. It was a beautiful sight to behold. Centuries of hate and anger had been replaced with love, peace, and joy, all in one day. Prime Minister Catlin had done it again!

A special meeting of the Confederation had been called for the following Tuesday, and Prime Minister Catlin insisted that Bishop John be allowed to attend. They had become inseparable, and Catlin wanted Bishop John there. Permission was granted making Bishop John the only outsider to ever attend one of their meetings.

The Confederation headquarters was the most elaborate building that had ever been constructed. Thousands of tourists would pass by annually just to catch a glimpse of the elegant edifice.

It stood on a high hill that overlooked a beautiful, flowing river, and was surrounded by golden gates that sparkled in the sun. It looked like a castle of splendor.

They were all assembled in the meeting room when Prime Minister Catlin and Bishop John arrived. Both men were greeted warmly, and Bishop John was asked to open with prayer.

The Bishop smiled, and proceeded with a few words to a god that warmed the hearts of all. After he sat down, the leader of the group, President Rosch, stood and called the meeting to order by recommending that they vote as to who would replace him as president. Another member quickly seconded the motion, and the voting began.

Again, it was unanimous that Prime Minister Catlin was to be the new President of the Confederation. Catlin stood up beside the former president as Rosch grabbed his hand and lifted it high in the air. He turned to the group and exulted, "President of the Confederation today, and President of the world tomorrow!" The rest of the men jumped to their feet as their applause filled the room.

The Prime Minister smiled his approval to all of the men gathered. The time had indeed come: he was going to rule the world. Pride welled up within him as he squared his shoulders back. He put his hand out to quiet the men.

"As you are all aware," he said, "the Middle East has recently experienced some major changes within their countries, leaving their economy somewhat unstable. With the recent developments of unity that have transpired there, I propose to you that it would be in the best interest of the world, if the

Confederation were to step in and assist them with the reconstruction of their temples."

They all agreed to anything that President Catlin said. The men again applauded Prime Minister Catlin at his outstanding ability to lead.

Bishop John took advantage of the moment, and asked permission to speak. "We know that Prime Minister Catlin is a man of great wisdom that we all deeply respect. I believe that it is up to us to set the precedent for the rest of the world to revere this honorable man of intellect. I suggest that we make a crown for the new President to wear, and that it should become a law that everyone from the countries represented here to bow in his presence. I submit to you that he be received as royalty, and that we in this room be the first to act upon it." The men nodded in agreement.

At that, Bishop John bent down on his knees and bowed his head in reverence before Prime Minister Catlin. The other leaders followed suit.

The Prime Minister arrogantly surveyed the men kneeling before him. He straightened his back up as he cherished the moment. Although there were only a few men bowing before him now, he knew that it was only a matter of time that he would be standing before multitudes down on their knees.

A sinister smile appeared on Catlin's face as his focus drifted off to the ceiling. He became entranced with visions of the future as he gloried in his own being. A lurid beam shone from his eyes as they reflected fiery red.

Deceived

19

It was once again time for Lana's regularly scheduled meeting with Satan. One of her biggest delights in going there was to cause havoc with Satan's henchmen. Throwing her weight around gave her pleasure, and made her laugh with the horrible screeching sound; she loved to display her rank over them.

She bolted past the guards, went right up to the gate and knocked. Even though she had been given a very special power that could enable her to walk right through, she would never dare to. She waited until Satan granted her permission to enter.

"Give me your report!" He commanded.

"Master, I have everything under control. Bishop John and the new Confederation President have worldwide respect. President Catlin was able to bring peace to the Middle East, with our help, of course," she said confidently. "We don't have to use the original plan of creating a universal catastrophe with a nuclear bomb because President Catlin and Bishop John are already ruling most of the world now. They will have the entire planet under their control very shortly.

"The Confederation is already operating with the computer chip that has been implanted in the hands or foreheads of the people. It is just a matter of time before we will have it implemented worldwide. We have the humans that we control positioned in every Christian group. There is peace everywhere, and everyone feels safe and secure with President Catlin in charge. Bishop John has full spiritual authority."

Lana continued smugly. "We have created so much confusion and division, that this worldwide revival to Christianity is dissipating, and Bishop John is winning the hearts of the people."

Satan smiled his approval to Lana. His eyes gleamed a fiery red as he listened with excitement to Lana's report. His master plan was succeeding, and it would not be long before he would rule the universe!

As if reading his mind, Lana diffidently asked, "Master, please tell me when you plan for us to enter into the bodies of Bishop John and President Catlin, so we can rule together?"

Satan stared right through her, "Be calm, Lana! *When the time is right.* They are doing a fine job right now, and we can still rule them from the outside.

"It won't be long, Lana. It won't be long."

Deceived

20

Jerusalem was a place of jubilation. The streets were filled with dancing and singing. All enjoyed general camaraderie as the joyful celebration carried on throughout the city. The Jewish people anticipated the day very soon when they would be able to worship in the new temple on the exact location of where the original one sat.

President Catlin was scheduled to speak to the nation. He no longer wore a suit and tie: he now clothed himself in a robe. The Confederation had honored him with a very elaborate crown. It differed from the one that Bishop John wore because Catlin's was full of precious stones and much larger.

The ground was still lying bare where the Dome of the Rock had been standing. One could actually see with the naked eye all of the intricate tunnels and passageways that had been hidden for centuries. The Ark of the Covenant was still sitting in one of the rooms, and remained untouched because the few that had attempted to secretly tamper with it lay lifeless just a few feet away. After that, no one dared to even approach it, not even to remove the dead bodies.

A platform was brought in for this special event, and thousands had gathered to hear President Catlin speak. They were pressed in, trying to get as close as they could. It was a multi-cultural crowd with Arabs and Jews all blended together.

As Bishop John approached the microphone to introduce President Catlin, the entire sea of people all bowed their heads in reverence. Because they were packed in so tightly, they were unable to kneel as they normally did in his presence. As the crowd raised their heads up, they saw Bishop John lift his arm toward heaven. Immediately fire fell from the sky and covered the temple site nearby. A wave of gasps sounded from the onlookers as they observed in shock. There was now solid ground covering the area, and the Ark of the Covenant was sitting on top!

It was a glorious site! Words could not describe the beauty. It sat there basking in the sun's rays with such brilliance that the people had to shield their eyes from the glare.

Lana stood there looking out at the crowd and at the miracle that had just taken place. She looked down at her new body in complete amazement! *"The time must be right!"* She thought as she turned around to look at President Catlin. *"Yes, the time is right – there he is, Satan himself! I would recognize those eyes anywhere."* Lana loved it.

Since Lana had chosen to appear on earth in the form of a woman, she realized that it would be different, living in a human male body, but did not care. It was the power, authority, and new position that was held next to Satan that mattered. *"Who knows? I might like this better,"* she thought to herself. *"Good-bye, Lana...Hello, Bishop John!"*

Now, Lana had been around when the Ark of the Covenant was first built, and she knew God's rules concerning it. Satan did too, so after she introduced him, the first words out of his mouth were, "Is there anyone present who knows, without a shadow of a doubt, that you are a direct descendant from the tribe of Levi?"

The crowd shuffled about as several men made their way through the packed audience and knelt before the two leaders.

President Catlin instructed them to retrieve the Ark, but they were not to touch it. Instead, they were to place special rods into the rings that were located on the sides of the Ark in order to move it. He then stepped down off the platform and over to the men. As he did, he held out his arms and the necessary rods appeared in his hands. The crowd gasped in astonishment.

The Prime Minister handed the rods to the descendants of the Levitical line of priests and told them to go. They were to march around the perimeter of the sacred ground before bringing it back to the platform.

President Catlin walked up the steps of the platform to where Bishop John was waiting at the top and they made eye contact with each other. Satan gave her a wink, and she gave him the "thumbs up" signal. No one else saw what had transpired between them.

Tim Blake was present providing international media coverage. The whole world witnessed as the Ark was finally brought forward onto the platform and the crowd went wild with enthusiasm. Everyone on the planet was totally captivated with the scene, and Prime Minister Catlin and Bishop John reveled in their glory.

One man suddenly ran forward in his excitement to touch the Ark. He was instantly thrown back about six feet and collapsed onto the floor. Several men rushed to his side, and then one man confirmed, "He's dead!"

President Catlin announced to the people that God was not pleased, and that *no one* was to touch the Ark of the Covenant. Fear fell over everyone watching; that is, except for the people of God. They knew what the Bible said was coming, and they knew what to expect.

JJ and Lynn were watching their TV from their living room. They were not fooled for a moment, as they shook their heads in disbelief.

JJ grabbed Lynn's hands and began to pray, "Heavenly Father, please open the eyes of all of your people, and show them the deception that is happening here. Give us all supernatural wisdom, knowledge, and the strength we need for the days to come. In Jesus' name, Amen."

Deceived

21

A young man darted like lightning up the platform stairs, drawing out the sword that he had hidden underneath his garment. He plunged forward, striking a fatal blow to President Catlin. Blood was instantly running down his beautiful robe and onto the platform, as he collapsed to the floor.

Bishop John screamed into the microphone, "That man is the anti-Christ!"

Some men rushed over, roughly grabbed the young man by the arms, and hauled him away as he kicked and screamed.

A doctor who was present in the crowd was summoned to examine the beloved President, who was still lying on the platform. The doctor bowed his head as his body began to shake in grief. "He's dead. He's dead," the doctor sobbed.

The crowd began to wail. Tim Blake's voice was immediately heard throughout the world on live television saying: *Nations of the world, President Catlin is dead.*

The camera crews then turned to show the doctor crying as he held the lifeless President, covered with blood, in his arms.

They wanted to take President Catlin's body away, but Lana discouraged it because she knew that it was just a matter of time before President Catlin would rise back up. Bishop John turned to the crowd and said, "Let us pray together."

The prayers were soft at first, but then grew louder and louder.

Tim Blake was in shock. This day had to be monumental in his news casting career.

About a half an hour had passed, as the television crews were constantly focusing back and forth from the Ark, to Bishop John, and to the dead President lying on the platform.

Suddenly, President Catlin's eyes opened. The doctor sat up, startled, as the President stood to his feet without any assistance. Everyone watched in amazement as the blood totally disappeared, and the wound was completely healed before their eyes. The crowds went wild.

Tim Blake thought to himself, *Journalism just can't get any better than this.* His camera missed the knowing look and the half-grins that were exchanged between Bishop John and the President.

President Catlin motioned for the crowd to be still, continuing on as though nothing had happened. "Today I am here representing the Confederation," He said. "We are making a treaty with Israel and the Middle East countries. Within this treaty, we are going to supply all of the finances and labor needed to rebuild their temples. Experts will be brought in to oversee the construction, and will be under the supervision of each country to do their commands. These temples will be erected very quickly with the Ark of the Covenant being housed in the same place as it was from the beginning."

President Catlin had captivated most of the world, and the people accepted his words. The Christians who knew the Word of God were keenly aware of what was going on. However, these two men who were bringing peace to the world and performing great miracles were misleading the new converts who had very little knowledge of the Bible. Now, the world was even more mesmerized since President Catlin's encounter with death, and his miraculous resurrection on live television. It was as successful as he had planned.

Lynn turned to JJ as they watched the television screen. She said fervently, "JJ, our work is cut out for us! We have to teach the new believers the Word of God, and quick! This deception is overwhelming! Let's get on the Internet and put on our website all of the scriptures that speak about what we have just witnessed. Let's do it right now!"

JJ nodded as they both rushed over to their computer.

Meanwhile, the meeting had finally come to an end as Bishop John and President Catlin were escorted off the huge platform. They went over into a nearby facility, and into a private room. As soon as the door was shut behind them, they both began to laugh and slap each other on the back with excitement. Bishop John did not feel the need to bow down to the President because he felt like he was on the same level with him.

The President shot both arms towards the ceiling in a sign of victory. Satan spoke to his demonic cohort through the President, "See what I told you? I have these stupid little humans eating out of my hands!" He roared even louder. "Deceit is my greatest tool, and it's so easy for me! I'm indeed the master of deceit!"

Deceived

22

A guard outside knocked on the door, interrupting Satan and Lana. "President Catlin, a little, old Jewish man is outside, insisting that he speak with you immediately concerning the rebuilding of the Jewish temple."

"Send him in."

The guard returned within a few minutes, leading a man wearing a large brim, black hat, and a button up suit. He appeared to be around seventy years old with a long white beard. He was small in stature, and soft spoken as he said, "President Catlin, I have been chosen by God to be instrumental in rebuilding the temple. I received this information in a vision that I had when I was twenty-four years old. I am very close to the people who have been preparing for this day for years. They have all of the vessels and necessary items ready that will go in the temple.

"The Jewish people have longed for this day," His voice faltered as he continued. "As a special request, I would like to be the one in charge of the rebuilding."

Bishop John and President Catlin looked at each other, and then back at the old man as the Bishop asked, "What is your name?"

"Benhadad."

President Catlin thought for a moment as he inspected Benhadad. He then responded, "Yes, I will put you in charge. Be aware of this, though, I want it erected quickly. Do you understand?"

He nodded fervently.

"I will furnish you with everything that you need. All of the material and labor will be at your disposal immediately."

Tears welled up in Benhadad's eyes as he held back the flood of emotions that overwhelmed his soul. He leaned forward on the stool on which he sat, and asked softly, "Mr. President, if I may ask one more thing?"

Catlin nodded.

"The Jewish people would like to re-establish their ancient ritual of the daily sacrifice. Would you grant permission for us to do that?"

"Yes, Benhadad. Go and tell your people that I will help in every way possible. Let them know that I am their friend," President Catlin said. "Get your temple built and get the daily sacrifices established. I want the world to know that there is peace in Israel."

"Sir," Benhadad said emphatically, "You will be surprised at how quickly this will take place. You see, everything is already prepared, even down to the stones that will be used in the building. We won't need any outside help because it is already prepared. You will be very satisfied with the progress my people will make."

Satan burst out, "Go do it! What are you waiting for?" He pointed to the door.

"I wonder where the President came up with the Ark of the Covenant that he just exhibited," Benhadad thought to himself as he exited the room. "We found the real one years ago, and have it hidden in a secret place. I can guarantee one thing – the one placed in our temple will be the *real* Ark of the Covenant, that's for sure."

After Benhadad was gone, President Catlin turned to Bishop John and asked, "How do you like my plan? We have deceived almost everyone into thinking that we are holy peacemakers. In a very short time, all nations will be bowing down to us, and that is the part I like the best!" Satan snickered. "Worship! I want the world to worship *me*!"

Bishop John thought to himself, "I'm liking this worship, too!"

Events began to move very swiftly on planet Earth. Within a few months, the Jewish temple was rebuilt on the original temple mount, and daily sacrifices were re-established. The Dome of the Rock had also been rebuilt not too far away. Music and dancing was continuous in the streets of Jerusalem.

All of the male descendants from the tribe of Levi had been located and brought to Jerusalem. They were the only ones who were allowed to perform the functions of the Jewish Temple.

The Jewish people were honoring God, and many were accepting Jesus Christ as their Messiah. President Catlin and Bishop John were well aware of what was going on, but decided not to interfere in order to maintain the peace. They could not afford to have any national and international problems now that they were established as the peacemakers.

JJ and Lynn, and the other committed Christians around the world were not taken in by President Catlin and Bishop John. They used the Internet to correspond and pray together, as they taught the new converts around the world the Word of God. They knew that the current events taking place were the fulfillment of Bible prophecy.

Deceived

23

A year had passed. During that time, the people of all nations had come together in one accord, and the entire world was at peace. President Catlin was no longer just the President of the Confederation, but he had become the leader of the *world* with Bishop John right at his side. Wherever they went, Lana (Bishop John) was able to perform great and mighty miracles because of the power that he received from President Catlin.

The temples had been erected in Jerusalem, and the Levites were conducting all of the traditional ceremonies that their ancestors did in the days of old.

The Confederation was the governing power for the world. Everyone had been registered into the

Catlin Computer Bank; and only those who had received the computer chip in their hand or forehead were able to buy or sell.

Earlier that year, late into the night, JJ and Lynn heard a knock at their front door. Figuring that it was someone in need of counseling, they made themselves presentable to receive their visitors. When they opened the door, two men were standing there.

"We have been sent from God Almighty, and are here on a very special assignment," one of the men began. "We have been told to come here, and to stay at your house."

Lynn immediately spoke up, "You are the two witnesses that are spoken of in the Bible, aren't you?"

The one with a rugged look smiled. " We were told that you two had very strong spiritual discernment, but we didn't expect you to recognize us so quickly."

JJ and Lynn warmly welcomed the visitors into their house. The four gathered around the dining room table, and Lynn served some refreshments. They stayed up for the rest of the night discussing their assignment for the end of the age. Over the next several months, the four of them became very good friends.

Deceived

24

The world President and Bishop John were in a very elaborate office that had been set up for them. They were puffed up with pride, boasting about their accomplishments when Satan stopped abruptly and grilled Lana about JJ and Lynn Murphy.

"You have nothing to worry about," replied Lana. "Their group has dwindled down, and they are not a threat to us anymore. I have a group watching them at all times. You can just forget about them.

"They have two house guests that occupy most of their time. The guests look really peculiar and wear funny looking clothes. They think that they are really spiritual by going around and prophesying to everyone. They spend most of their time with the Murphy's flying back and forth to Jerusalem."

"You are lying to me, and I know it!" Satan declared through President Catlin. "These two men, along with the Murphys, *are* a threat to us, and we *are* going to do something about it.

"I have held this back until now in order to bring total peace to the earth. *Now, the time is right!* We are going to rid the world of every follower of Jesus Christ," President Catlin said as he pulled out a sheet of paper from his desk and handed it to Bishop John. "Here is the list of things that I want done immediately."

Bishop John took the sheet of paper and read over the listed items:

1. Do away with the tax credit that churches receive.

2. Ban all meetings that don't worship me, even the ones meeting in homes.

3. Everyone is to worship my image; kill those who don't.

4. Burn all of the Bibles inspired by God because we now have our own worldwide bible.

5. Make sure that no one can buy or sell anything without the computer chip.

6. Execute anyone who is found helping those without the computer chip.

7. Get rid of all Christian web sites.

8. Make sure that everyone believes that they are doing God a favor by getting rid of all of the Christians.

9. Too many Jews are beginning to believe in Jesus Christ. Break my covenant with them – stop the daily sacrifices.

"Also," President Catlin said, "Find out who these two house guests are of JJ and Lynn Murphy."

Bishop John nodded his head in agreement as he jotted down that last command. They looked at each other with understanding.

"Now go to work: I am getting sick of being with you all of the time," President Catlin blurted out. "The Murphys will not agree to take the mark, and they will not bow down to my image. This is the way that we can legally get our hands on them. As soon as they are arrested, send for me. I want to be the one to take care of those two. They will pay for what they did to me in Washington D.C." His eyes filled with rage as he planned his revenge.

Claire Hollis, Ph.D.

Deceived

25

God's holy remnant of true believers of Jesus Christ were being persecuted and killed in the months to follow as Satan's commands were being performed. JJ and Lynn were eventually arrested, and President Catlin was notified.

He had been waiting a long time for this day. As he marched down the hallway to where the Murphys were being held, onlookers could see the hatred shooting from his eyes. Catlin roughly turned the knob of a side door, and entered into the room.

JJ and Lynn were seated at a table in handcuffs. JJ spoke, "We know who you are, Satan, and we know where you are going to spend eternity."

President Catlin raised one eyebrow as he glared at JJ. His teeth clenched behind his tightly closed lips.

"We also know where we are going to spend our eternity," JJ continued. "You may now have the power to kill our bodies, but you can't touch our souls. If you kill us, you will be doing us a favor, because to be absent from this body is to be present with the Lord. We aren't the least bit afraid of you. We know that your power is soon to come to an end!"

Satan was completely silent as he glared with hatred at JJ. He shook his head, as he wrung his hands together. "We'll see about that," he hissed. "I understand that you have eight children and nineteen grandchildren. You two will be executed tomorrow at noon, but first…"Satan paused as he narrowed his eyes at them."You will witness all of your children and grandchildren being tortured and murdered before your eyes!"

A wicked grin appeared on his face, before he began to chuckle. A hideous blast of laughter that could be heard throughout the entire building quickly followed as President Catlin turned and swayed cockily from the room.

Lynn and JJ sat motionless as if someone had stabbed their hearts with a dagger. Lynn began to cry.

"JJ, you know that there are some of them who are not right with God," she sobbed. "What can we do?"

"Let's pray, Lynn. God has never let us down, and He won't now."

Lynn nodded in agreement as JJ began to pray, "Heavenly Father, we want you to know that we trust you no matter what..."

Some guards entering into the room interrupted him before he was able to say another word. JJ and Lynn were lifted up by their arms and escorted out the door. They were led to different cells where they remained separated. They stayed awake all night praying for their children and grandchildren.

Morning dawned much too quickly, and the Murphys were brought before President Catlin. All of their children were huddled there in the room, whispering to one another. Satan was in his glory as he was finally getting the ultimate revenge against these two. He was seated on a big throne that had been placed on a platform in the center of the room. JJ and Lynn were brought onto the platform allowing them a good view of their children below.

Satan demanded the attention of everyone in the room. He said, "Nobody in this room has a computer chip. If anyone would agree to be stamped with one right now, then I will allow you to go free." He turned to JJ and Lynn. "That includes you two as well."

Two of the children started to walk forward to receive the chip when several reached out and pulled them back. They quickly whispered to each other in another family huddle. Several of them had little ones crying in their arms.

Finally, they rose up out of their huddle and the oldest son spoke for the group. "We have all made the decision to follow Jesus Christ, and we have all prayed for God to forgive us of our sins. We are all willing to give up our lives for Him. We are ready to die.

"Mom and Dad, thank you for leading us in the right direction, and for setting the right example. We want you to know that we love you very much. We know that Jesus is real because we have seen Him in you."

JJ looked over at Lynn. Their eyes met, and they knew the joy of what each other was feeling. This had to be the most glorious day of their entire lives', knowing that within just a few minutes, the entire family would together share eternity with Jesus Christ and with each other.

Satan's eyes fixed on Lynn. His eyebrows seemed to come together as he frowned. His square jaw line was set. After staring at her for a few minutes, he asked, "Is there anything that you want to say? Do you want to change your mind? I'll make you a deal...if you receive the computer chip, it will not only save your own life, but also everyone in this room. What do you have to say for yourself? Do you really love these kids, or not?"

Lynn took a deep breath as she stared evenly back at Satan. She began to speak in her soft voice, "You couldn't touch me unless God allowed you to. I trust God and His decisions. The greatest desire of my entire life is to see all of my children come to the Lord and to be fully committed to Him. My deepest desire has just been fulfilled. President Catlin, *you have just made my day!*"

Satan's fury was out of control. He grabbed the guard's laser gun, and within minutes, everyone was lying on the floor. He threw the gun down and ran from the room. All that was left, heaped on the floor that day, were the Murphys' lifeless bodies. The guards who were left to clean up the mess could not see the twenty-nine angels who flew into the room to quickly escort the spirit and soul of each family member away to their heavenly eternal home.

The Murphys were all wearing white robes, and smiling at each other. They were all laughing together, winking at each other, and sending each other victory signals with their thumbs up, as they expressed exceedingly exuberant joy. It was a celebration that was never going to end.

The news of the Murphy family assassination reached their two house guests. They were furious with President Catlin. One of them spoke up, "Soon and very soon, we will show him our power, and he won't be able to touch us!"

The other one agreed. *"When the time is right!"*

They were both aware of the power that they had over the whole earth, but their time had not yet come.

President Catlin screamed as he left the Murphy family in a pile on the floor. He screamed, and screamed, and screamed. His revenge had turned sour, and he was mad. JJ's words kept ringing in his ears: *...We know where we will spend eternity...we know where you will spend yours!*

He couldn't stop the words. They were replaying over and over in his brain like a tape player.

Satan was so depressed over losing the victory with the Murphys that he summoned Lana. He grabbed her by the hand, and they went straight to Jerusalem. This time they didn't use the conventional way on a jet; Satan was in too much of a hurry. He had to do something to get rid of this depression. The only way he knew to be happy was to be worshiped, and he didn't want to share that with God.

They stopped only long enough to pick up a statue of President Catlin. They marched into the Jewish Temple, knocking down all of the Jewish priests dressed in their robes. They went directly into the Holy of Holies, walked over to the Ark of the Covenant, and kicked it onto its side.

Satan then slammed the statue of himself down where the Ark once stood. He lifted his hand toward heaven, shaking his fist in God's face. He then spit on the Ark.

God Almighty was sitting on His throne in the splendor of Heaven as he watched what was taking place. Jesus was there with him seated on his right side. The Father turned to Jesus and said, "Better get ready, Son... *It's almost time!*"

Warfare Plus Ministries, Inc.

Claire, and her husband Paul, minister nationally and have seen thousands of people freed from demonic influence. They each hold a degree of Ph.D. in Clinical Christian Psychology, and conduct private and group counseling sessions. They also conduct seminars and teach a School of Deliverance.

Other books from Warfare Plus Ministries

THIS MEANS WAR! - A complete guide to the teachings of Christ on deliverance, along with many other biblical references regarding deliverance. Sadly, deliverance has been treated almost like a forbidden topic in the church realm. THIS MEANS WAR! teaches in great depth everything you always wanted to know about demon warfare and the supernatural, but have been afraid to ask!

DEMON SLAYERS - Actual case histories of people who have gone through deliverance. Relive the experiences with them as this book takes you through shocking, extreme, intense battles of Good versus Evil—and Good always prevails!

Warfare Plus Ministries

Product Number	Description	Quantity	Unit Price	Total Cost
BOOKS				
WP-101	This Means War		$12.95	
WP-102	Demon Slayers		$11.95	
WP-103	The Light		$11.95	
WP-104	Delayed Invasion		$11.95	
WP-105	Deceived		$12.95	
AUDIOS				
WP-201	Expose & Expel Demon Power (4 Tapes)		$20.00	
WP-202	Inner Healing/Spiritual D. (4 Tapes)		$20.00	
WP-203	Don't Get Caught In Satan's Web		$10.00	
WP-204	Are You Cursed? (2 Tapes)		$10.00	
WP-205	Power & Authority Over Evil (2 Tapes)		$10.00	
WP-206	If I'm Supposed To Be Gay …(2 Tapes)		$10.00	
VIDEOS				
WP-301	Expose & Expel (4 Videos)		$80.00	
WP-302	Inner Healing/Spiritual D. (4 Videos)		$80.00	
WP-303	Deliverance From Satan's Torment		$20.00	
WORKBOOKS				
WP-401	Expose & Expel Demon Power		$20.00	
WP-402	Inner Healing/Spiritual Deliverance		$20.00	
WP-403	New Beginnings In Jesus Christ		$20.00	
			SUB TOTAL	

Method Of Payment:
- ☐ Visa
- ☐ MasterCard
- ☐ Check

Credit Card Number: _____

Expiration Date: _____

Shipping & Handling
$10.00 & Less	$3.00
$10.01-25.00	$4.00
$25.02-40.00	$5.00
$40.01-60.00	$6.00
$60.01-75.00	$7.00
$75.01 or more	$9.00
USA RATES

Shipping & handling (see chart)	
TOTAL	

Please Print Clearly

Name _____
Address _____
City _____
State _____
Zip _____

Send To:
Warfare Plus Ministries
4577 Gunn Highway, PMB 206
Tampa, FL 33624

Fax: (813) 908-0228
E-Mail: WarfareP@aol.com